D1084780

ALSO IN THE PARIS HOMICIDE SERIES

THE 7TH WOMAN

**Best Crime Fiction Novel of the Year
(*Lire* Magazine)**

**Winner of France's most prestigious
crime fiction award,
the Prix du Quai des Orfèvres**

An international bestseller

"Blends suspense and authentic police procedure with a parallel tale of redemption. Well-drawn characters and ratcheting tension."

—Paris mystery writer Cara Black

"Molay uses meticulous police procedure and forensics to bolster gripping scenes of terror. Let's hope more installments from this series cross the ocean soon."

—*Booklist*

"A taut and terror-filled thriller. Frédérique Molay creates a lightning-quick, sinister plot. Inspector Nico Sirsky is every bit as engaging and dogged as Arkady Renko in *Gorky Park.*"

—*New York Times* bestselling author Robert Dugoni

"A slick, highly realistic, and impeccably crafted thriller."
—*ForeWord Reviews*

Praise for

Frédérique Molay

and

Crossing the Line

"This is a spellbinding procedural, with an appealing protagonist and a fresh setting... procedural fans will appreciate the fresh take."
—Booklist

"Frédérique Molay is the French Michael Connelly."
—Jean Miot, Agence France Presse (AFP)

"The kind of suspense that makes you miss your subway stop."
—RTL

"An excellent mystery, the kind you read in one sitting."
—Lire

"A fast-paced story that you don't want to end."
—Nord-Eclair

"Another adventure full of suspense with a personable hero and a brisk investigation."
—Chroniques Littéraires

"Molay has the art of leading us through the streets, cafés and hidden places in Paris, and she knows her police procedure like the best of them. A treat to read, truer than true. The pace is perfect."
—Polar collectif

Crossing the Line

A Paris Homicide Mystery

Frédérique Molay

Translated from French by Anne Trager

LE FRENCH BOOK ▮

All rights reserved: no part of this publication may be reproduced or transmitted by any means, electronic, mechanical, photocopying, or otherwise, without the prior permission of the publisher.

First published in France as
Dent pour dent
by Librairie Arthème Fayard
World copyright © 2011 Librairie Arthème Fayard
English translation © 2014 Anne Trager

First published in English in 2014
by Le French Book, Inc., New York
www.lefrenchbook.com

Copyediting by Amy Richards
Proofreading by Chris Gage
Cover design by Jeroen ten Berge
Book design by Le French Book

ISBNs:
978-1-939474-14-8 (Trade paperback)
978-1-939474-15-5 (E-book)
978-1-939474-16-2 (Hardback)

This is a work of fiction. Any resemblance to actual persons, living or dead, is purely coincidental.

To my dear children.
To those I love, here and elsewhere.
To Zira and Cornélius.

Now, mystery I love passionately, hoping each time to unravel it.
—Charles Baudelaire, Paris Spleen

PROLOGUE

With a trembling hand, the man set down the tiny piece of plastic. He had found a way to get a message to the right people. It had to work. He studied the words he had written. How odd to contemplate a future he wouldn't be a part of. But he wasn't dead yet, and he would do everything he could to protect his loved ones.

§ § §

1

Nico Sirsky breathed deeply, concentrating on his stride. His arms were bent at ninety degrees, and his eyes were focused straight ahead. The harsh cold bit his cheeks, but he kept a good pace, pain notwithstanding. He had been shot in the leg a few months earlier, and he was still recovering from the injury. The endorphins raced through his body. The effort felt good.

A Radiohead album given to him by his son, Dimitri, hammered his ears. The hit "Creep" brought his thoughts back to Caroline. "You're just like an angel. Your skin makes me cry... I wish I was special. You're so fucking special." This morning, she was already at Saint Antoine Hospital, where she ran the gastroenterology department. Nico had gotten up and gone for a run when she left. The exercise helped him chase away the ghosts of those he had locked up and their ravaged victims. This curious moment at dawn, between night and morning, put him in a parallel universe. The glow of the city dazed him with its dance of headlights, streetlamps, window neon, and floating strings of Christmas decorations setting the trees ablaze. The silent forms that crossed his path went from shadow to light before disappearing around a bend or into a subway entrance. Everything seemed unreal, and with the music, he felt as though he were racing through a movie set. There he was, an extra amid overall indifference, belting along as if the devil were hot on his tail.

Nico had started his jog at the Esplanade des Invalides, skimmed around the Eiffel Tower, circumvented the Arc de Triomphe, and made his way along the Champs-Élysées to the Concorde. Then he ran past the Tuileries Gardens and the Louvre. His next milepost: the Luxembourg Gardens. He could hear Commander David Kriven, one of the Criminal Investigation Division's twelve squad chiefs, teasing him about how ridiculous it was to take the right bank to get from the Invalides to the Sénat. There were more direct routes and certainly less strenuous means of transportation than on his one good leg.

It had been only three months since the surgeon had operated on Nico's leg. After that, he had dived into intensive physical therapy—there was no way he would concede the slightest victory to the bastard who had targeted him. Nico had braved it all, even if it meant clenching his teeth and swallowing painkillers. Spread the word: Chief Nico Sirsky was back full time in his fourth-floor office at the Paris police headquarters, 36 Quai des Orfèvres. He had returned to his old brown-leather chair and his giant worktable filled with case files and police complaints. He was once again leading his team of a hundred or so elite crime fighters. Just as important, he had put his stormy divorce and the sudden departure of his depressed ex-wife behind him. He had custody of their fourteen-year-old son, and now Dimitri, Caroline, and he were a real family.

In the middle of the Pont des Arts, Nico felt transported to a snowy scene in Russia, his family homeland. The roofs resembled mountaintops in the Caucasus. In front of him, in place of the golden dome of the Institut de France—home of the Académie Française—he imagined the red façade of Moscow's Saint Basil's Cathedral. Nico smiled at the thought of Paris strutting its stuff, no matter the weather. Come rain, wind, or snow, his city revealed all her finery with the same charm, like an experienced, elegant, and spellbinding woman. The Seine River rippling beneath him complemented the magic.

Returning to the Left Bank, Nico slipped on a thin layer of white powder that carpeted the pavement. He recovered his footing just as he felt his phone vibrate in his pocket. Who could be calling at such an early hour? Going by probability alone, he guessed it was headquarters. Like a praying mantis lying in wait for its quarry, death stalked the city's alleys, dead ends, and gardens in the hours before dawn. And the most pious-looking killer could strike at dizzying speed.

Caroline's name appeared on the screen with a text message. "I love you. Be careful." Nico felt a knot in his throat; never before had he had such strong feelings for a woman. "Luv U 2," he answered as he sped up, running in pace with the sensual harmony of The xx, with its distant guitars and troubling blend of refinement and brutality.

He finished with a sprint down the Rue Oudinot. He typed in the gate code and pushed his way into a small private alley lined with a few handsome homes. This was his corner of paradise, near the Tour Montparnasse. He entered his house and took off his sopping-wet running shoes. In the hallway, a note was hanging from the coat rack: "Hi, Dad. Hope you're okay. Off to school. Later. D." Nico looked at his watch. It was seven thirty. He sighed and went upstairs, in great need of a hot shower. The water spurted out, calming him, and Nico imagined Caroline's gentle hands soaping him up, her mouth glued to his.

"Stop that, would you!" he said out loud.

He rinsed quickly and stepped out of the shower, wrapping a towel around his waist and going into his room—their room. Caroline had kept her apartment but came here more and more often.

Nico put on a suit and tie and then unlocked the safe at the back of the closet. He grabbed his holstered gun and felt its weight in his hand. Friend or enemy? Life or death? A gun protected as much as it threatened. As he attached it to his belt, the cold, hard reality struck him again. He hated having to use his gun, but like so many other things in this world—crime, separation, illness, loss—he had to deal with it.

A half hour later, Nico turned onto the Quai des Orfèvres. The faux-medieval tower of police headquarters rose up alongside the Seine. He parked in his reserved spot next to the building. Security guards saluted him with deference as he entered the cobblestone passageway that led to the interior courtyard. He felt ready and alert, as if he were going into a stadium. He walked along the outside wall until he reached the glass door to Stairwell A. The headquarters were cramped and in a sorry state, but the police prefect was working hard on a plan to move the operations to a new building in the Batignolles neighborhood. Despite the additional space and better conditions the new quarters would offer, Nico was not thrilled about leaving 36 Quai des Orfèvres. He liked the old-fashioned feel of the building, with its stairs covered in black linoleum and crumbling hallways haunted by the ghosts of his illustrious predecessors.

On the fourth floor, a lit sign that looked like it belonged in a train station signaled the hallway. In dark blue letters on a white background, it read Brigade Criminelle. It was La Crim', otherwise known as the Criminal Investigation Division. At the entry to the hallway, a showcase held merchandise sold to support the Police Benevolent Association. The mugs, key rings, caps, T-shirts, and Champagne were all branded with a thistle, the elite division's emblem. The division's slogan was posted on the wall: "Brush against us and you get stung." There was no ambiguity in those words.

Nico gave a few instructions to his secretaries and headed down the hallway to his office, one of the few on the floor that was large enough to be comfortable. The mandatory portrait of the president of France welcomed him. The furniture was outdated, but the space was pleasant enough and offered a breathtaking view of the Seine. He barely had time to sit down in his large leather chair when the phone rang. It was Claire Le Marec, his deputy chief. She was a competent police officer who had skillfully taken over for him while he was in the hospital, preserving his higher-ranking position and never trying to grab the spotlight.

"We're ready when you are," she said, referring to Nico's daily meeting with his four section chiefs to review their active cases. Before, they would have knocked on his door and entered without any ceremony. But Le Marec continued to serve as a buffer, perhaps out of guilt for not having been there three months earlier, when a murderer had spread terror throughout the city, challenging Nico and trying to kill both him and Caroline.

"You've been slaving away these last few weeks, Claire. Lighten up. I'm not made of eggshells. The proof is in my running shoes, which just flew over six miles of sidewalk and are begging for more."

"See. You're already overdoing it."

Nico smiled. "Come on. I bet I could outrun Yann anytime." Claire's husband was from coastal Brittany and good at sea but inept on land. "I'm waiting for you," he said, his tone professional again. He hung up, lost in thought. He knew he was no more invincible than Captain Amélie Ader, one of the six members of David Kriven's squad. Ader had been murdered by the serial killer who had targeted Nico. The case had burst the bubble of protection that he had thought surrounded those close to him just because he embodied the police force. It had never really existed.

No Christmas elf could change that.

2

Dr. Patrice Rieux walked quickly along the Rue des Saints-Pères, which bordered Paris Descartes University. He glanced down an alley to a door that led to a grimy basement. Students found the ghoulish atmosphere in the basement perfect for hazing. Broken cabinets, decrepit work surfaces, dented water basins, burst file boxes, and battered carts were scattered all over the floor. A confusion of pipes covered the ceiling, like snakes ready to drop and bite under the dull fluorescent light. Not a place for the sensitive soul.

A little farther along, at 45 Rue des Saints-Pères, a group of young men, cigarettes between their lips and deep circles under their eyes, milled at the entrance, stamping their feet against the cold. Dr. Rieux passed a large pine tree and made his way into the university's main hall. He squeezed through a crowd of students, most of whom would never make it beyond their first year. They were overworked, tired, and pushed to their limits. The dentist climbed to the sixth floor. A yellowing piece of paper taped to a glass door pointed to the anatomy department. It was past the body donation office. A grim waiting area was reserved for those who were willing to give their bodies to science after they died but had questions while they were still alive. The area consisted of a small wooden bench against a wall. Posts with unrolling straps closed off a nine-square-foot zone. The space was almost always empty, as if sitting there could bring bad luck. Actually, the bench had an aura of death.

The legendary red door at the end of the hallway opened with an ominous creak. Marcel appeared in the hallway in his usual outfit, which was like a second skin: jeans, immaculate white coat, and plastic clogs. He was short and heavyset, with thick hands, white hair, and a sharp eye. The man was a good sixty years old, and the red door was his. It led to his own private suite next to the Farabeuf Lab. Marcel was the most experienced body processor at the university. It was best not to know his production secrets.

Patrice Rieux greeted him warmly at the entry to the lab. Marcel said hello, his blue eyes sparkling with mischief, and then he reassured the dentist that the specimens were ready.

Inside the lab, forty or so dentists were jostling at the buffet table for coffee, fruit juice, and pastries before putting on their uniforms. In his tailored nineteen-seventies-style floral shirt, the kind he wore when he haunted these halls as a student, Dr. Rieux clearly enjoyed playing host. And he now frequented this place regularly, thanks to the postgraduate training clinic run in partnership with the university. His company offered a full anatomy and pathology course of studies for practicing dentists who wanted to perfect their emergency surgery skills. The coursework was practical, and the techniques were taught on fresh subjects—fresh, but dead. Dr. Rieux had hired a team of teaching-hospital practitioners and private-practice dentists to oversee the students. They wore white coats and name tags. The students were in single-use smocks, shoe covers, and blue caps.

Patrice Rieux entered the classroom and felt the usual shiver run up his spine. He loved being in this temple of medicine. Temple: there was no better word for it. The ceiling was nearly twenty feet high. Huge shuttered windows towered above the blackboards, and a giant screen rose up in the front of the room. Fluorescent fixtures as big as bathtubs diffused a uniform white light over the twenty-four dissection tables lined up in four rows. The environment was perfect for surgery, which offered an emotional ride one hundred times more exhilarating than a roller coaster. Contrary to popular belief, doctors did not think of themselves as all-powerful gods. They were too aware that the slip of a needle or a minute scalpel error could endanger a patient's health and even a patient's life. Wasn't that fear of making a costly mistake indispensable in this profession? The job required extraordinary concentration, unwavering energy, and comprehensive knowledge.

This day's patients, however, did not need such crucial attention.

While his colleagues checked the equipment, Dr. Rieux greeted Professor Francis Étienne, head of the anatomy department at Paris Descartes University. The man was planning to retire, which was bad news for the students. Étienne was a master in human anatomy and organ topography. He knew exactly where to slice into the flesh so that it left barely a trace. But cemeteries were filled with irreplaceable professionals, all of whom had wound up being replaced.

The professor grinned at Dr. Rieux. He was nearly quivering with excitement: a fish in his element. "I'm ready," he said.

A lab tech stood next to the professor, ready to hand over instruments and aim the operating lamp. He also had the task of running the camera so the students could follow the procedure on the screen.

The metallic sound of trolley wheels on the floor tiles signaled Marcel's arrival. Silence fell in the Farabeuf Lab, and the room felt a few degrees warmer. In one quick, smooth gesture, Marcel whisked away the large blue sheet that covered the stainless-steel cart, and all the students looked away. The heads of twenty men and women of all ages stared out. The decapitations had been done according to the rules of the art, and the body processor had acquitted the task with skill. Marcel started handing out the specimens, setting them on holders on the tables, next to surgical instruments and rolls of paper towels. The students took their places at their assigned tables. Professor Étienne prompted his assistant to start the camera and zoom in on the head he had been given.

"This morning, Wednesday, December 2, we'll be focusing on mandibular wisdom-tooth surgery," the professor began. Our specimens here are a bit unusual, in that they still have their wisdom teeth. As you know, many people have had these teeth removed by the time they are in their mid-twenties."

The tech inserted retractors to hold the jaw open, and after a few jokes, the room hushed.

"Let's start with the lingual flap. Ladies and gentlemen, by freeing up this part, you avoid damage to the lingual nerve just inside the mandible. One wrong movement with the drill, and half the tongue goes numb. Now that would be awkward, wouldn't it?"

A few students chuckled.

"Okay, let's continue. Please pick up a number fifteen scalpel, and we'll start by cutting into the cheek," Professor Étienne said as he made the incision on his head, which was then magnified on the screen. "Make a sulcular incision like this."

The room was perfectly quiet. The students were entirely focused, as they leaned over their heads.

"Cut the membrane and part of the buccinator muscle upward toward the front edge of the mandibular nerve branch. Now take a periosteal elevator, and free the gum from the periosteum. Done?"

The teaching team, led by Dr. Rieux, roamed up and down the rows, commenting and helping out.

"Now make a vertical incision with Metzenbaum scissors."

"Gently, gently," Dr. Rieux said. "We're not cutting steak here."

Light laughter relaxed the atmosphere.

"You now uncover the entire bone on the vestibular side, preserving the buccal nerve and making sure the patient still has feeling in his or her cheek. *Voilà,* you've done it." He worked quickly and smoothly, his hands steady from years of practice and perhaps the assurance that his patient was no longer capable of sensing any pain.

"Let's move on to the next step. Do the same sulcular incision on the tongue side. Free up the tissues. When you see the wisdom tooth, introduce your Metzenbaum, and open from front to back and then from the vestibular to the lingual."

"That's easy to remember," a dentist at one of the tables whispered. "First you open the vestibule, and then you give it some tongue."

"Do you have something to share?" the professor asked. "Look at the screen, my dear man. The lingual nerve—it looks like a big strand of spaghetti—is in the flap. We'll now use a Tessier convex-shaped blade to protect the nerve so you can drill the bone and cut out the tooth without damage to the mandible."

Dr. Rieux stopped at a table where two students were working diligently. "Perfect," he said.

"This guy has great teeth," one of the students said. "He obviously takes care of them. He doesn't have many cavities. And his dentist does excellent work. Look at those composite resins and onlays."

"You mean he *took* good care of them. In case you haven't noticed, all he's got left is his head."

"Yeah. This is weird, though," the second student said. "His front teeth are cracked. And do you see that big mercury filling in the back molar? Don't you find that strange for someone who looked after his mouth so well?"

"We're not plastic surgeons," Dr. Rieux said.

"And look here. There's something sticking out of the filling."

"What? Let me take a look," Dr. Rieux said, leaning in to examine the tooth. He picked up a scraper and poked at the object. "Hmm. We'll ask Marcel to set this head aside. We'll take a drill to it and find out what that tooth is hiding. I'm sure it's nothing. For now, though, it's time for a break. Let's go to lunch."

The dentists set down their instruments and took off their masks. Some let out sighs.

"I believe that Dr. Rieux has planned a delicious meal for us," Professor Étienne called out from the back of the class.

"That's right. I'll meet you all in thirty minutes on the Rue Saint-Benoit. It's right around the corner. I booked tables at the Petit Zinc. You'll love the décor."

"And the lamb shoulder with Lautrec pink garlic," Étienne added.

The dentists applauded the morning's session, and the room filled with the hubbub of squeaking stools, snapping latex gloves, and buzzing voices. The professionals then made their way into the sixth-floor hallway, where they mixed with younger and louder surgical interns spilling out of the Poirier Lab. The result was a good-spirited clamor.

The dentists found themselves outside in the winter cold. Christmas was a few weeks away, and Paris was covered with snow. The sky was one of those pewter grays captured by Pieter Bruegel the Elder in Renaissance paintings, and the air was filled with the aroma of hot roasted chestnuts offered by street vendors. The sights and smells brought a festive allure to the capital, as shoppers, their arms full of gifts to place under their Christmas trees, rushed in and out of stores.

The Petit Zinc was a delightful example of Art Nouveau, called *style nouille*—or noodle style—by its detractors because of its pasta-like swirls and curls. The dentists were transported back to the Belle Époque, into a warm and magical atmosphere far from the stainless-steel dissection tables.

Dr. Rieux clapped to get his colleagues' attention. "The chef has prepared some fine dishes for us today. We'll start with a salmon melody, gravlax style, and follow that with chorizo-larded cod steaks and mashed potatoes."

Professor Étienne interrupted. "But nothing beats their lamb shoulder."

"Francis, admit that I'm doing you a favor. I could have ordered the veal's head, but I think we've had enough noggins for the moment. For dessert, there's bourbon vanilla crème brûlée. We'll have a cabernet sauvignon with that, served at the ideal temperature of ten to twelve degrees, Celsius, of course. There's no risk of killing anyone today, but don't overdo the wine. A little respect for the dead, please."

The group laughed, as other restaurant patrons looked on.

"One more thing before we start eating. Unfortunately, Marcel won't be able to join us. I had to excuse him. Without him, nothing that we do within the walls of that university would be possible. His work with the dead serves the living, as we all know. So before we pick up our forks to taste this delicious marinated fish, let's raise a toast to him."

In unison, they raised their glasses of wine.

Meanwhile, Marcel was at work on the sixth floor. Time was ticking away. He needed to process the bodies for the afternoon and could spare only a few minutes to wolf down a sandwich—ham and butter on a fresh baguette.

There was deep silence all around. It didn't bother him. He was used to working alone, removed from the living. In the Poirier Lab, surgical interns had opened up the abdomens and stitched them closed on the batch of subjects he was now loading onto trolleys. Some of them had been used so often, they would be sent to the incinerator. He took them back through the red door, which was off limits to the public. Behind the door, he had three walk-in cold rooms, where the bodies were stored on metal shelves. Although the rooms were large, the ceilings were low, and the lighting was poor.

Next, he attacked the heads in the Farabeuf Lab. He'd have to replace some of them, the ones that had been through the hands of student ophthalmologists and neurologists and were in a pitiful state. He set them out in his lab, which resembled a small kitchen, with a portable stove, pots, a sink, and a coffeemaker for long nights and days that started when the rooster crowed. He placed the overused parts in a large pot of water and brought it to a boil. He would simmer the contents until the flesh fell off and nothing but bone was left. The skulls would be used for lecture classes. In the meantime, Marcel prepared a dozen upper limbs that the European School of Surgery had ordered. He amputated the inert arms at the shoulder. The class would focus on the elbow joint.

When he finished, he returned to the Farabeuf Lab to put out some new heads. He stopped for a moment to study the one Dr. Rieux had asked him to set aside. It belonged to a man who was probably forty or so years old. He was rather handsome and most likely well off, which was clear from his shiny white teeth. The cracks in the front teeth and the horrible filling ruined it all. The filling was especially strange. All the others were the same color as his teeth. Marcel took a closer look at the thick gray amalgam. Something was sticking above the surface by a tiny fraction of an inch. He hadn't noticed it before the dentists started working on the head. Their manipulations had probably jarred it into view.

Marcel couldn't resist. After all, he was responsible for the bodies. He plugged in the drill. A quick run at forty-two hundred revolutions per minute was all it would take. Despite his large, powerful hands, Marcel was skilled at minutia. He turned on the instrument, and it made the familiar whirring sound that caused the living so much anxiety. He began to dig at the molar. The filling slowly crumbled—until the bit became ensnared in a tiny piece of cotton. Marcel stopped the drill, grabbed a little scraper, and explored. Inside the cotton, he discovered a minuscule piece of meticulously folded plastic.

Marcel pulled it out with a pair of tweezers. Then he sat down on the nearest stool. He had seen much in his career, but nothing like this. It had to be some kind of joke, or the man was very smart. Marcel looked him in the eye.

"Just what I thought," the body processor said.

He pulled out his cell phone. "Dr. Rieux?"

"Speaking." There was talking and laughing in the background.

"Marcel here."

"Oh, Marcel. We're sorry you're not with us."

"I haven't been wasting my time, doc, believe me."

"What's that you said?"

"I said that if I were you, I'd get back to the classroom on the double."

"Is there a problem?"

"It's possible, yes. Nothing I can explain over the phone. You'll have to see it in person."

"Okay, I'm on my way."

"And ask your friends to take their time. Tell the restaurant to serve up an extra coffee."

Dr. Rieux ended the call without another word. Marcel knew the doctor would be on his way faster than a rabbit. Now he had to call his boss, Elisabeth Bordieu.

She answered on the third ring. "Yes, Marcel, what is it?"

"I've got a problem in the lab."

"Did something else break down?"

"No, nothing like that. But I think you should come see this. We're going to need you."

3

Deputy Police Commissioner Michel Cohen, his signature cigar in his mouth, knit his brows and looked Nico in the eye. He was short—five feet four inches—but he imposed his authority. "I'm counting on you. The prefect is impatient. He's got the media on his tail, and the interior minister breathing down his neck. His job is on the line, which means our jobs are on the line. Understood?"

Six months earlier, thieves had pulled a heist at a jewelry shop on the Avenue Montaigne. They had gotten away with eighty-five million euros in booty, an absolute record in France. The police hadn't yet caught the thieves, which was embarrassing the interior minister. After all, this member of the prime minister's cabinet was responsible for the country's security and law enforcement. Naturally, the interior minister was putting heat on the prefect, whose job was coordinating the police force.

Now, headquarters was under the gun. Nico understood this all too well. The media would jump all over the slightest mistake, and heads would roll. The first to go would be the prefect. Nico wasn't eager to see that happen.

"We're on top of it," Nico said. "We've intercepted the jewels the thieves hawked. We'll catch them soon. It's a matter of hours."

"There's no time to waste," Cohen said. "We need to act now."

Nico nodded. His boss wanted arrests. That morning, he had discussed the case in detail with Deputy Chief Jean-Marie Rost, one of his four section chiefs. He led the investigation squads headed by commanders Kriven, Théron, and Hureau. Rost had fine-tuned the operation hand in hand with the Organized Crime Division. Nico was confident. They had proof that the security guard at the jewelry store had participated in the holdup. The guard had been killed after the robbery, but thanks to him, they had tracked down the brains of the operation. All they had to do now was to catch the fish. They were cunning fish, but they were within reach.

Deputy Chief Rost was calm, despite the dark circles under his eyes, his pallor, and his unpredictable moods. These days he went quickly from wearing a silly smile, which his colleagues teased him about endlessly, to looking stressed and preoccupied, as if something were eating away at him. The explanation was simple: Jean-Marie Rost was a new dad. As the father of a one-month-old baby, he was facing a life full of surprises and emotion that were worth more than those eighty-five million euros. It was enough to make anyone wiser and more committed.

Michel Cohen walked slowly across the room, leaving a smelly cigar trail. At the door he turned and gave Nico one of his trademark winks, a sign of encouragement. In moments like these, he looked like a movie rendition of a mob boss from the nineteen twenties. It was a rather incongruous image.

Nico dived back into his case files. The Avenue Montaigne heist was not his only concern. His job had an inexhaustible supply of crimes and misdemeanors.

His phone rang. It was the police commissioner's secretary.

"Chief Sirsky? Commissioner Monthalet wants you in her office. Now."

"I'll be right there."

He trotted down Stairway A to the third floor. A uniformed officer monitored access from behind a large window and control screens. She looked up from the mystery thriller she was reading and greeted Nico as he walked through the doors. He continued past the offices of Nicole Monthalet's chief of staff, a charming man who had once been a police commander. These days, he called himself the minister of propaganda and master party organizer. It was his job to buff the division's image.

Nico opened the door that had just been painted red—a color befitting Monthalet's authority and power. It led to a freshly renovated sitting room with bright white walls and hardwood flooring. An elaborate bronze chandelier hung from the ceiling. To the right were Cohen's office and another office for the head of the Bureau of Information, Statistics, and Criminal Documentation. Straight ahead lay Monthalet's antechamber.

Nico walked down the hall to Monthalet's office. The door was wide open.

"She's waiting for you," one of the secretaries said.

Forty-five years old, Nicole Monthalet had short blond hair and dark brown eyes. She was wearing a gray pantsuit and gold earrings with black-diamond settings. Her only other jewelry was a simple wedding ring. She had natural class.

"Sit down, Chief. You know that Paris Descartes University is one of France's flagship medical schools, right? It's also an important research institution, and the school's president is a friend of the interior minister. I've attended functions with them. Well, the president of the university has contacted the interior minister about a very strange case. It must be handled with care. I don't want him coming down on us. You've been handpicked to deal with it."

Nico noted the half smile on his boss's lips.

"It already looks like a case that could go down in the textbooks," Monthalet continued. "It may be a bad joke, but be forewarned, it could also get a lot of unwanted attention. Very unwanted."

Nico didn't react. Monthalet would soon show her cards. She was drawing out the suspense, but perhaps not for the fun of it. She looked disconcerted. That surprised Nico.

"Dental students at the university were working on some heads, and one found a foreign object in a molar. At lunch, a tech drilled the tooth and pulled out a piece of plastic with a message on it."

"What did it say?"

"I was murdered."

Nico was silent. Now he understood.

"The public prosecutor has ordered a preliminary investigation. If it's a prank that went bad, I want to know right away. This case takes precedence. Make it go away."

Nico opened the door to the Coquibus Room, where Commander David Kriven's squad had its office. A large poster of Henri-George Clouzot's 1947 movie *Quai des Orfèvres*, with Louis Jouvet playing Inspector Antoine, hung on one of the walls. None of Kriven's detectives were even born when the movie came out, yet they personified the emblematic police characters in the film. Nico couldn't help noting the timeliness of the poster. *Quai des Orfèvres* had unfolded on a snowy Christmas Eve.

Kriven sprang from his chair. The fair-complected commander with raven-black hair was like a big cat ready to give chase at any moment.

"You get to stretch your legs," Nico said. "Orders from the prosecutor. You're coming with me."

Of the division's twelve squads, nine of them—which handled homicides, kidnappings, missing persons, sex crimes, arson, and other sensitive cases—were on call every ninth day. Kriven's squad was on.

Captain Pierre Vidal, the third-ranking detective in the squad and the one in charge of processing the crime scene, grabbed his field kit. He and his assistant would collect and document the evidence. At the back of the room, under the window that looked out on the Seine River and the Pont Neuf Bridge, an overflowing ashtray sat on a radiator. That was Vidal's doing. Nobody held him to the rules. He had started smoking again after Captain Amélie Ader had been slain. A mint-scented air freshener barely masked the odor. Vidal and Nico gave each other a knowing look, one that said, "We will get better; every day is a little bit better."

Nico settled into the passenger seat. David Kriven turned up the heat and pulled into traffic. He was intent on the road, swerving past pedestrians and cars and barely staying off the sidewalks as they drove along the Seine. At the sight of the flashing lights, other drivers pulled aside. Snowflakes hit the windshield, forming stars like those that would soon hang from Christmas trees. Nico allowed his mind to wander for a moment. He was thinking about what he would give his son, Dimitri, his mother, Anya, his sister, Tanya, her husband, and their two children. And then there was Caroline. She gave this Christmas even more significance. He had a family that meant everything in the world to him—a family that he had wanted to draw even closer since his brush with death. He wanted to do something that would express his feelings in a way that required no words.

They arrived at the nearby Rue des Saints-Pères in no time. It reminded Nico of his days at the prestigious Paris Institute of Political Studies—Sciences-Po. At the time, he already wanted to take the officer's exam and go to the national police academy. It took him months to tell his father, who headed a business empire and wanted his son to take over one day. Anya had been forced to issue an ultimatum. If he didn't tell his father, she would, which would surely make the man even angrier. So, with sweaty palms and a heart fighting its way out of his chest, Nico had faced the man. The blood had drained from his father's face. He stood up without saying a word and grabbed a glass and a bottle of Spiritus, a gut-burning Polish alcohol. He poured it and downed the drink without blinking. Nico hadn't dared to move until Anya stormed into the room, put the bottle away, and laid into both of them.

"You're both idiots. Nico, you're not ten years old anymore. Take responsibility for your choices. If you want to play cops and robbers, that's up to you. My life will become hell. I'll wake up every morning praying that nobody shoots you in the head and will go to sleep every night thanking the Lord that you are still with us. But what counts is that you are happy. As for you," Anya continued, pointing at her husband, "you're just acting like a bully. Tell him what's in your heart. That's the only thing worth saying."

His father cleared his throat. He hesitated, then finally said, "I love you, son" and took Nico in his arms.

"Good. Case closed," Anya proclaimed, leaving the room.

She had always been theatrical. Nico had pursued his dream of becoming a police officer and chasing criminals. But that didn't stop him from helping his father from time to time, and they had brokered some fine business transactions together before his death.

Commander Kriven drove through the gates at 47 Rue des Saints-Pères, the entrance reserved for service vehicles.

A woman who looked about sixty years old was waiting for them. She was shivering in the cold, despite the winter coat wrapped around her.

Nico got out of the car and held out his hand. "Chief Sirsky from the Criminal Investigation Division."

"Elisabeth Bordieu, administrative manager of the Body Donation Center," she said, shaking his hand and looking impressed.

Nico was used to his position having that effect and also knew that his six-foot-two stature, blond hair, and blue eyes made an impression on women.

"This is my team. Let's hurry. You don't want to catch cold."

She led them into a vast gray garage where merchandise of all types was loaded and unloaded, from food to school supplies, manuals, equipment, and furniture. Two light-colored wooden coffins sat in a corner. The group's footsteps on the concrete floor echoed as they made their way to the large double doors. Elisabeth Bordieu gave them a hard push. On the other side, a steep ramp led to the basement. There was no noise, and the silence in this seemingly secret passageway was both fascinating and chilling. A rusty freight elevator took them to the sixth floor. Its cables creaked the whole way. Clearly, this university had seen better days.

The elevator let them off at the end of a long hallway. The red door at the other end caught their attention. A sign indicated limited access. Nearby, two rooms faced each other, the Poirier and Farabeuf labs.

Elisabeth Bordieu stopped and said, "I don't exactly know where to start."

Nico gave her a reassuring look. "You can start by telling us where the head is."

"Marcel, one of our body processors, brought it back into his workshop. We have a heavy schedule this afternoon, and we couldn't hold up the anatomy lab."

"Is that the same Marcel who drilled into the tooth and found the message?" Nico asked.

"Exactly. During lunch hour."

Kriven glanced at his superior officer, as if to say there were better ways to spend a lunch hour.

"He's in charge of the subjects, and he's a perfectionist," Bordieu said, clearing her throat.

"The subjects?" Nico asked.

"The anatomy subjects. The deceased, if you prefer. We don't refer to them as dead bodies here," she continued.

"I understand," Nico responded. The choice of words depended so much on who was talking. Anatomy subjects, dead bodies; tomato, tomahto.

"Some courses require only certain anatomical parts," Bordieu went on.

"That would be heads for the dentists, in this case."

"That's right. They are still working in the Farabeuf Lab. But orthopedic surgeons might need hands or elbows."

Clearly, her job meant a lot to her. Nico was sure that Elisabeth Bordieu knew everything there was to know about "anatomy subjects" and didn't keep nine-to-five hours. He admired her. But if he were to listen to his ex-wife, he admired women's qualities and capabilities a little too much.

"I suggest that Captain Vidal and his assistant, Lieutenant Almeida, examine the head."

"I'm not sure that… Well, I mean the workshop is rather off-putting, to say the least, and generally only the processors go in there."

"Don't worry. These are seasoned detectives. Nothing behind that door could shock them, and the information they gather is privileged."

"I'll let Marcel know, then."

"Yes, it's best that he be there. In the meantime, three of my men will question the dentists."

Nico gave the signal to the detectives in the squad in charge of canvassing, and Kriven's new assistant, who had replaced Captain Ader.

"Commander Kriven and I will stay with you, Mrs. Bordieu. We need to understand how your department works, how the head ended up here, and, most of all, who it belongs to."

4

Nico and Kriven sat down at the round cherrywood table in Elisabeth Bordieu's office. A secretary brought them three cups of coffee. A large window looked onto the snowy Paris rooftops and the occasional swirls of chimney smoke.

"So you are in charge of body donations. What is the relationship with the university?" Nico asked.

"The Body Donation Center is a full-fledged department of Paris Descartes University. Our mission is research and teaching, and we work under a professor of medicine—he's a distinguished neurologist—and his assistant. There are four units. The administrative unit has four processors, two secretaries, and myself. The other three are the scientific council, which approves research and handles publications, the ethics committee, and the video unit, which offers courses via video conferencing in France and abroad. In some countries, body donation is forbidden, which makes it difficult for surgeons in training."

Elisabeth Bordieu seemed organized and methodical.

"So, is your department the only one authorized to accept bodies that arrive here at the university?" David Kriven asked.

"That's right."

Nico sipped the warm coffee. "Did the head we're here to inspect come from a body donation?"

"It did. We receive 650 bodies a year, on average, which represent a third of the donations made in France. Ours is a major donation center."

"What procedures do body donors have to follow?"

"Donating your body to science is something like writing a will. What I mean is that it must be voluntary and documented. Anyone interested in doing so must provide a handwritten, signed, and dated letter stating his or her intention."

Bordieu walked over to her computer, and the printer spit out a sample letter, which she handed to the detectives. It felt like a foretaste of death. He wondered what motivated those who would agree to sign over their bodies. What would he do?

"Why?" he asked.

Bordieu focused on him. "For more than forty years I've been working with dead bodies, to use the term I detest. It's a profession quite unlike any other. I'm surrounded by exceptional people whose only ambition is to improve the lives of others. And even with all my experience, I still wonder why people donate their bodies to science. Maybe it's to ensure that science keeps progressing. Maybe it's to feel like they are helping others after they die. I imagine that in your job, you have your fair share of questions. Why do men kill, Inspector?"

As Captain Pierre Vidal went through the red door and entered the domain of the body processors, he could still hear his boss's words. "These are seasoned detectives. Nothing behind that door could shock them." Well, he got that wrong. Vidal had smelled plenty of blood in his career and had seen many mutilated bodies. But this was something else altogether. It was much more insidious. His legs felt weak, and the pressure in his chest was making it hard to breathe.

The acrid, fetid stink of the dead struck him first. That was followed by the smell of chemicals and bleach. The room was cold and damp. Faucets with hoses lined the hallway off three large cold-storage rooms. Through windows in the doors, he could see the bodies piled up and cut up like pieces of meat.

Lieutenant Almeida's face had gone pale, and Vidal was concerned that he might faint. What sissies we must look like, he thought. Marcel, however, was in his element and clearly excited about the police being there.

He led them to his lab at the end of the hallway. There was the head, staring at them, its mouth open.

"Shit," Almeida said. The lieutenant took out his digital camera and started taking pictures from all angles.

"What's that?" Captain Vidal asked as his slipped on a pair of nitrile gloves, which he used instead of the regular variety because he was allergic to latex.

A number was written in black pen on the forehead.

"His name," Marcel said. "Let me introduce 510."

"Nice to meet you, 510," Vidal responded.

"Don't be offended if he doesn't say hello. He's lost his voice," Marcel said with a chuckle.

"Has anyone touched him?" Vidal asked.

"Of course, but always with gloves."

"Who?"

"Me, the three other people who work here, the dentists in the Farabeuf Lab, ophthalmologists, neurologists."

An eyelid had been sewn shut, and there were stitches running behind the left ear.

"He's still holdin' up well," Marcel said, looking proud as he gazed at his body-free ward.

"We're going to have to take it off your hands," Vidal said. "It's evidence now." Almeida pulled out a lamp with colored filters. Ultraviolet light uncovered fingerprints. Violet was for blood, and blue and green were for fibers, urine, and sperm. In this case, it was hard to find anything useful, because the body fluids could be from anyone in the building.

"Was the head preserved in the cold room?" Vidal asked.

"Yes, at thirty-nine degrees. That allows us to work on the parts for about a month. I freeze the bodies at minus four degrees when necessary, and that way we can keep them for several months."

"Where's the rest of 510?"

"I thought he'd be better off in the fridge. I gotta warn you, students in digestive surgery had a crack at him this morning. And Italian orthopedic surgeons worked on his arm. When docs are learning some techniques, it's best not to work on living subjects, so they come here."

"This head, 510, seems awfully pale."

"Normal. We wash the head to get rid of blood and other substances before it gets any kind of injection."

"You mean injections to color the arterial and venous systems? What technique do you use?" Vidal asked.

"Green latex suspension. After washing, I inject an ammoniac solution that keeps the latex from hardening too fast. Then the needle goes into soapy water, and I fill the syringe with the magic potion and do the injection in one fell swoop. When the latex hardens, it's easy to dissect the part, because the vessels keep some of their flexibility. That's the advantage."

"You know a lot about this."

"It's my job. I pamper them."

"Where is the message you found in the tooth?"

"Here, in this tray. It says, 'I was murdered.' Blows your mind, doesn't it?"

Vidal used tweezers to pick up the piece of plastic. He slid it into a numbered evidence container. He added the date, time, place, and his initials. The police had to follow strict conservation and tracing procedures for any evidence to hold up in court. Almeida was taking samples for a DNA test they would do later. Then they started examining the mouth.

"The message was hidden there, in that filling," Marcel said.

As Vidal examined the filling, something caught his eye, something the dentists hadn't pointed out. It was a new element in the case. And a big one.

"Why would someone give his or her body to science?" Elisabeth Bordieu repeated the question. "It might be because the person is alone, or doesn't have any close family members, or wants to spare the family the burden of dealing with a funeral and all the ceremony. And there is also the feeling, as illusory as it is, of staying a little bit longer in the world of the living."

Commander Kriven cleared his throat and asked, "Once the person writes the official donation letter, what happens?"

"When we receive the letter, we send a donor card," she said, holding out a sample. "Death to serve life" was written on the back. The orange card detailed the proce-dure to be followed when the donor died.

"I presume you have some, well, losses," Kriven said.

"That's true. Not all the bodies make it to us. There are quite a few reasons for this. We need to get the body within twenty-four hours, or forty-eight if it's kept in cold storage. Sometimes it takes longer than that to get here. Sometimes the relatives are not aware of the arrange-ments the deceased has made. There are also families that refuse, overriding the person's wishes. Sometimes the relatives can't find the donor card, or the donor changed his or her mind and destroyed the card without informing us. The other possibility, which is the exception, would be some legal obstacle, such as a suspicious death."

"Well, our head made it here," Kriven said.

"That means that a doctor signed a mandatory non-contagion certificate specifying that the donor didn't have any communicable disease, and the family gave permission for incineration."

"What happens then?" Nico asked.

"The family pays an accredited private transport company to deliver the subject. It can be an undertaker or a specialist who works with us. The body is dropped off at 47 Rue des Saints-Pères. Then a special elevator takes the body to the sixth floor, where your colleagues are right now. The processors start by taking blood and tissue samples. The secretary fills in admission forms, and the body is registered. It gets a bracelet with the donor's number, age, and blood-test results."

"Just like at the hospital when you have a baby," Kriven said.

"A poet once wrote, 'We shall not cease from exploration. And the end of all our exploring will be to arrive where we started and know the place for the first time,'" Bordieu said.

"That was T.S. Eliot," Nico said.

"I'm impressed. I like the poem, because it relates to what we do here. By allowing physicians and students to examine the dead, we can help them learn about life. As for the specifics, each subject gets a number, which is written on the thorax, forehead, and each limb. We keep the bodies in cold storage. Sometimes we embalm them, which allows us to keep them for a whole year. It all depends on who has reserved what. I'm directly responsible for the scheduling. Our students use these subjects, as do students from the European School of Surgery, which is housed in this building. Other institutions, like physical therapy schools, give courses on the premises too, and there's continuing training. We have four dissection labs and some smaller research rooms."

"What happens to the bodies afterward?"

"They are put in coffins and transferred to the Joncherolles crematorium in Villetaneuse, where they are incinerated anonymously. The ashes are then scattered in Division 102 of the Paris Thiais Cemetery. There is a small marker so that families can visit."

"What number was our head?"

"Number 510."

"Can you guarantee that we can trace it?"

"Of course."

"So you'll be able to bring together all the parts belonging to the body?"

"We keep track of all the body parts, and we've already brought Number 510 together. Marcel handled it himself. He's the most qualified processor in the department."

"I have no doubt that your system is very efficient, but I have to ask these questions."

"You must understand. I love my job, and it's important to me that it all runs smoothly and that we treat the subjects with respect."

"So I gather," Nico said. He gave her his most reassuring smile. "You mentioned anonymity, which is an essential element in body donation."

"It's necessary, and that is what donors want."

"Yet you know their identity."

"It's registered in a notebook. My successor will certainly prefer computerized records, but I'm old school. The notebook contains all the donor information, and it keeps track of where all the body parts go."

"So let's get down to the key question. Who is 510?"

There was nothing reassuring to the detectives in the Farabeuf Lab. It was huge but oppressive. "Death is different every time you look at it," Captain Franck Plassard said to himself. "You can eat the same dish a hundred times, and it never tastes the same, just as no crime ever resembles another, and there's no getting used to it."

Surrounded by twenty decapitated heads, Plassard was sweating under his coat and hat. He was nauseous and felt a headache coming on. The windows were covered, the shutters closed. No daylight seeped in. The fluorescent lights gave the room an end-of-the-world aura. The clock on the wall had stopped, its hands frozen for good.

Professor Francis Étienne continued his class. The detectives looked at the screen and watched him cut from the ear to the top of the cheek and then down. He started pulling the skin away, as though he were doing a face-lift. He slipped the instruments in, pointing out yellowish, vile-looking fatty tissue and the ramifications of the facial nerve.

"Trim off the fat," he instructed his students.

Plassard held back a gag. He was used to autopsies, but seeing the same procedure done at the same time on twenty decapitated heads was like watching a horror movie.

"This is the same laboratory arrangement that we had this morning," Dr. Rieux whispered to Plassard.

"Where was the head?" the detective asked.

"On that table."

They walked over to two students who were focused on scraping the yellow layer from their patient's cheek. It was an older woman with a double chin and sparse gray hair.

"These are the two who found the piece of plastic sticking out of the filling," Dr. Rieux continued. "We were going to drill the tooth when we got back from lunch, but Marcel did it during the break. He called me immediately and then contacted Elisabeth Bordieu. We came back, and Elisabeth got on the phone with her director, who talked to the president of the university himself. You know the rest."

"What do you think about this?"

Dr. Rieux shrugged. "It's kind of crazy, you have to admit," he said. "Is it some medical student prank? Everyone knows that they joke around. Did you ever hear about the hands in the metro?"

"No, I can't say I have."

"That was when I was a student. A bunch of hands were found tied to a rail in the Mabillon metro station. They came from this school. Nobody ever found out who did it. Funny, isn't it? Today, a student who did that kind of thing would be expelled, out of respect for the subjects. I remember one day, too, when a janitor came face to face with a breast pinned to a wall."

"So you like that kind of joke, do you?"

"I didn't say that, but these anecdotes are part of the history of this place. I'm pretty sure that this morning's message will go down in the annals."

"So let's hope it's just a joke."

Elisabeth Bordieu set her record book down on the table and opened it carefully. It had twelve columns specifying date of arrival, number, first and last name, age, sex, date of death, transporter information, geographic origin, lab results, how it was used, and incineration date. Nico focused on a column with the heading "W."

"What does that mean?" he asked.

"Whole. It means it arrived as a complete body."

Bordieu ran her finger down the page to Number 510. "Bruno Guedj, age forty-seven. He died on November 20 in Paris and arrived here on the same day."

Now 510 had a name. And he had been dead for twelve days.

"We need his full file," Nico said.

Elisabeth Bordieu nodded and was reaching for her phone when someone knocked at the door. "Come in," she called out.

Captain Vidal stuck his head in.

"Can I see you for a second?" he asked.

"I'm coming," Nico said. "Kriven, get Mr. Guedj's file." Nico stepped into the hallway.

"I have something, Chief."

"What's that?"

"It definitely doesn't look like 510 died from natural causes."

5

Back in the calm of his office, Nico thought about the Locard Principle. "Every contact leaves a trace." That had come from Edmond Locard, the father of French forensic science, who was often called the Sherlock Holmes of France. Criminals always left evidence. Provided there were a criminal and a crime. That was a question they would have to answer quickly to keep the powers above them happy.

"Let's talk about Vidal's discovery," Nico said.

"Vidal found a wound measuring about five millimeters in the palate, showing all the characteristics of a gunshot wound," Commander Kriven said. "There is no exit, so we can presume the projectile is lodged in the skull. The head shows no other sign of violence, other than that done by the medical and dental students."

"Logically, that would make this a suicide," Nico said.

Deputy Chief Rost raised an eyebrow.

Nico continued. "Several conditions must be met before the university will accept a body. The death cannot be suspicious, and it cannot be the subject of an ongoing investigation."

"Generally speaking, any death involving a firearm is investigated," Rost said. "If it's a suicide, a ruling is usually made fairly quickly, and the body is released to the family. In this case, it would have been released to the university."

"So we're to believe that there was nothing suspicious about the death that would have led to an autopsy," Kriven said.

"Elisabeth Bordieu mentioned a certificate of noncontagion that must be signed by the physician who declares the death. Did she give you a copy?" Nico asked.

"The certificate was signed by Dr. Philippe Owen, a first responder."

"Question him as soon as you can. I'll go with Vidal to the coroner's office to attend the autopsy. Professor Armelle Vilars will be doing it tomorrow morning."

"What do we know about the victim?" Rost said.

"Bruno Guedj, forty-seven years old, residing at 10 Rue Roger Verlomme in the Marais," Kriven said. "Profession unknown—that part of the donor form is optional. Note that his donation letter is dated October 14, which was just five weeks and two days before his death."

"So he had a feeling," Rost said.

"We can be sure of one thing," Nico said. "A shooting death means the police were involved. We need to contact our colleagues in the third arrondissement. Their report will give us some more information. Then we'll question his family and colleagues."

"What kind of man would hide something like that in his tooth?" Kriven asked.

"The university dentists say it's a professional job," Nico said. "We'll need to find the dentist who did the filling."

"What about the message? Did Bruno Guedj write it himself?" Rost asked.

"Forensics has it now, along with the letter Bruno Guedj wrote on October 14, and the lab will compare the writing," Kriven said.

Nico wrapped up with a warning. "The media love sensation, so when they get wind of the message, it'll be all over the news. If this is a joke, let's find out before word leaks out. That will please our bosses, which, as you know, is especially important now."

Rost and Kriven nodded. There was no time to lose.

Nico paid another visit to the commissioner. Nicole Monthalet was leaning over a pile of papers, apparently trying to catch up on her casework. The bureaucracy was part and parcel of police work. And it was seen every day in the endless documents, reports, and other forms that had to be read and signed. They bounced from one office to another like Ping-Pong balls.

"Tell me everything, Chief Sirsky."

Nico sat down and summarized the situation. His superior officer leaned back in her chair and listened. When he had finished she said, "What do you make of it?"

Nico cleared his throat. "If this were a medical school prank, it would cause a lot of trouble for those who did it. And a suicidal man generally isn't in the mood for jokes. If that message really did come from Bruno Guedj, he felt threatened, and his death proved him right."

"I agree. But it is still too early to jump to any conclusions. In any case, the prosecutor wants answers. We'll know more tomorrow, right?"

Then she nodded, indicating that she needed no more from him.

Back in his office, Nico leaned against the window frame. It was already dark outside. The lights on the Place Saint-Michel and the riverboats exacerbated his feeling of isolation. He felt as if he were on a ghost vessel somewhere between the sky and the sea. The Christmas decorations, the thin layer of snow on the riverbank, and the bundled-up pedestrians reminded him that the holidays were dangerously close. He sighed and took out his phone.

"Hello?" The voice on the other end was thin and high-pitched.

"Jacqueline, it's Nico."

There was a long silence. It wasn't hostile—he had always gotten along with the parents of his ex-wife, Sylvie. Instead, it seemed filled with despair.

"Jacqueline, I haven't had any news from Sylvie. I'm worried. And I wanted to tell you and André that you will always be Dimitri's grandparents. He's missed you these last weeks, and since Christmas is coming…"

He heard sobbing and felt a knot in his throat. He had made the right decision. They agreed that the couple would spend a whole day with Dimitri the coming weekend.

"We'll take him out to eat and to a movie. Then we'll go shopping. We have time to make up for," Jacqueline said.

"He'll be happy. I'm sure of it."

"Nico, I understand why you might resent Sylvie. She hasn't always done the right thing. But she's our daughter, our only child."

His mother-in-law talked quickly, as though she had held in the words for some time and was now trying to unload them. It wasn't easy to admit that one's only child was unstable. Nico wondered if Dimitri's looks, so much like his own, had bothered her, as they had bothered Sylvie. Sylvie had also been jealous of her son's attachment to him. She had ended up sinking into a depression, taking medication morning and night, and finally running off and abandoning Dimitri.

"I would like to ask a favor of you, if I may," Jacqueline said quietly. "Of course, you can say no. I'd understand."

Nico knew what it was. "I'm listening."

"Please find our daughter. Find her. I can't help but think the worst has happened. I can't sleep anymore."

Wasn't that what he wanted too? To find her?

"I'll try," he promised.

"Don't tell André. I beg you. I don't want to build up his hopes."

"Okay, I'll keep you informed."

"Thank you," she said in barely a whisper before ending the call.

Nico left headquarters and headed back to his place. Caroline greeted him at the door and gave him a kiss.

"How about spaghetti for dinner?" she said, stepping aside so he could come in.

"Perfect."

He set his things down and looked at her. He felt all the emotions he had experienced when they first met. He was drawn to everything about her—her gaze, her smile, her soft voice, her firm body. He took a deep breath.

"I called Jacqueline tonight, and she asked me to do something for her."

"What's that?"

"She wants me to find Sylvie."

After a moment of silence, Caroline said, "I'm only half surprised. She must be worried out of her mind. What did you say?"

"That I would try. And Dimitri will spend part of the weekend with his grandparents."

Nico filled a pot with water and set it on the stove.

"So why are you hesitating?"

"I think I prefer sticking my head in the sand."

"It's time to pull it out. You need to do that. That's what Dimitri needs. And that's what we need."

Nico squeezed Caroline's hand. Then he wrapped his arms around her and inhaled her perfume. He slipped his hands under her sweater, shivering at the touch of her soft skin. His breathing accelerated. He pressed his mouth against hers, impatient.

Caroline pulled away. "Uh-uh. Dimitri is coming down."

"Why don't you come live here? Full time," Nico threw out.

"Indeed, why not?"

Nico gulped. Almost instantly, the jolting realization that the dream could fall apart—one freak on the street was all that it would take—paralyzed him. The thought was unbearable.

Dimitri appeared, took one look his father, and asked, "Are you okay?"

Nico turned to his son and spoke in Russian. "Yes, I'm fine, son. I asked Caroline to come live here with us. You and I have already talked about it."

Dimitri concentrated for a few seconds as he registered the words of his family's former tongue, and his face lit up. He answered in Russian. "What did she say?"

"Maybe."

"Don't look so worried. That's great!"

Nico felt genuinely happy, both because his son thought it was a good idea and because they had spoken in the language of their ancestors. They had been taking classes together with a friend, Iaroslav Morenko, who taught Russian at the Sorbonne. The man was an inveterate ladies' man who admitted that his accent helped a lot. Women loved the feeling of being swept into a James Bond movie, coming that close to the bad guy. Perhaps that was additional motivation for Dimitri, Nico thought. In any case, Nico couldn't wait to see Anya's face when Dimitri wished his grandmother a merry Christmas in her native language. He bet there would be tears.

"Hello. What about a translation?" Caroline said.

"It's man talk," Dimitri responded, pouring himself a glass of soda.

"I'll take some of that," Nico said.

6

Nico made his way across the Pont d'Austerlitz to the Quai de la Rapée and pulled up at the medical examiner's office. He had just finished his morning meeting with his squad chiefs, and there was electricity in the air. The net they were planning to drop on the Avenue Montaigne jewelry thieves was in clear view. In a little less than thirty-six hours, Deputy Chief Rost would lead Théron's and Hureau's squads, alongside the Organized Crime Division, in several raids in the capital and the surrounding region. They were all counting on surprising the criminals. There were no cowboys at headquarters. One misstep, and the whole operation could go haywire. They had lost cops for less.

The medical examiner's red-brick building was in a location bounded by the Seine River, the Quai de la Rapée, and line five of the Paris metro. Captain Vidal was waiting for Nico at the main entrance. Although it was cold, and Vidal was shivering, he seemed to be enjoying his cigarette. Nico watched him crush the butt with his heel and then pick it up with a tissue and slip it into his pocket. Vidal was incorrigible, the perfect crime-scene investigator who never left any evidence behind.

"Not a word," he said, frowning.

"I was thinking about your wife and how she must enjoy the mouthful of benzene when she kisses you."

"She's used to it. I've always been on fire," he said with a wink.

Nico chuckled and pushed open the doors to the sacrosanct temple of the dead.

"Chief Sirsky, sir," the guard said. He gave Vidal a nod. "Professor Vilars is waiting for you."

Armelle Vilars's office looked like so many other upper-management spaces in Paris. It was filled with old furniture and piles of files. The wood floors creaked. Vilars had bright red hair and a sensuality that made it easy to forget that she was the city's chief medical examiner, that prosecutors from all over France and even foreign countries relied on her, and that few dared to question her authority. If one did forget, the microscope with a slide holding a slice of some human organ colored with solution was the telltale reminder.

"Three thousand bodies come through this building every year, and I've personally performed over ten thousand autopsies since the beginning of my career, but this is the first time I've seen one from the Body Donation Center."

"Happy to give you a fresh challenge," Nico said.

She smiled and winked at Nico.

"Commander Kriven sent me Dr. Philippe Owen's observations. He was the physician on call with the paramedics," she said. "He noted a bloody nose and periorbital bruising. Basically, a black eye. It probably came from the shock wave. His examination revealed a small cranial fracture, which could be seen under the scalp. All these elements led him to determine death by firearm, the shot penetrating the mouth without perforating the skull, as there was no exit wound."

"Easy enough," Pierre Vidal said.

"Not really. Dr. Owen made his determination without examining the mouth cavity. The victim's jaw was, in effect, locked. A half hour to three hours after death, the jaw muscles contract, making it impossible to open the mouth. Rigor mortis actually starts with the eyelids and the mandible, spreading to the rest of the body in six to twelve hours and then disappearing in about forty-eight hours. Dr. Owen had the victim transferred to the nearest hospital. X-rays confirmed the presence of a conical foreign body lodged in the bone at the level of the left occipital area. My colleague concluded that it was a suicide. I imagine that the weapon was found near the victim and that tests for gunpowder residue came back positive."

Nico understood from her tone that she believed Dr. Owen's conclusions were a little hasty.

"Let's take a look," she suggested. "I asked one of my medical examiners, a specialist in gunshot wounds, to join us."

Nico and Vidal followed her through the hallways, passing a number of staff members, all of whom greeted them cordially.

"Has the family been informed of this new development?" she asked.

"Not yet," Nico said.

"I'll be here for them, if you think it is necessary. Just let me know."

While Professor Vilars was changing in the locker room, the two detectives washed their hands and slipped on their shoe covers, jackets, and masks. They didn't say anything. In this mythic place, the reality of death and violence filled the air.

Professor Vilars led them into the autopsy room, her green waterproof smock rustling. Looking like a clone, her colleague followed them in. Vilars and the gunshot wound specialist took up their positions near the stainless-steel dissection table, scalpel, bone cutters, saw, and cranial lever at hand. Nearby were recipients for organs that would be removed and weighed.

The chief medical examiner glanced at the wall clock and began recording. "We are beginning the autopsy of Bruno Guedj on Thursday, December 3, at 10:30 a.m., in the presence of Chief of Police Nico Sirsky and Captain Pierre Vidal, of the Criminal Investigation Division."

She slowly removed the sheet that covered the body. Nico had to suppress an urge to step back. Bruno Guedj was not in the best shape, and he smelled bad. Nothing like the stiffs on TV, with their hair and makeup done.

"The body was first examined at the Paris Descartes University by the crime squad," Vilars continued from behind her mask. "This examination revealed a suspicious wound inside the mouth characteristic of a firearm injury, with no other traces of violence. All other evidence was dismissed, due to the number of times the victim had been manipulated in the medical school and the state of decomposition. The postmortem time frame was confirmed to be twelve days. The medical examiner's office received the body in three distinct parts: the head, the upper right limb, and the rest as a single piece."

Nico focused on her words to distance himself from the scene as much as possible. Many experienced cops had fainted here, collapsing on the immaculate tile floor. It could happen to anyone. But this decapitated body, cut up and reassembled under the operating lamps, was like a Surrealistic painting. Nico glanced at Vidal, who seemed to be keeping his composure. He steeled himself. After all, he was no stranger to autopsies.

"We'll start with the head, the main piece of evidence."

After taking X-rays to identify any foreign objects and fractures, the gunshot wound specialist confirmed the existence of a bullet. Nico was an old hand at autopsy jargon and understood that diffuse dilacerations meant the bullet had disseminated tiny metallic particles along its path. The particles were in the brain tissue.

The external examination produced nothing more. There was a small cranial fracture resulting from the impact of the bullet and traces of the postmortem operations done at the medical school. Before focusing on the mouth, the medical examiner removed a sliver of the scalp and some hair for a later DNA examination.

"Do you see what I see?" Vilars asked her colleague.

"Yes, small fractures in the enamel on the right central and lateral teeth, both upper and lower. Our man broke his teeth."

"How's that?" Vidal asked.

"He could have bitten into the gun," Nico suggested.

"It's too early to tell," Vilars said.

"The bullet entry wound is round, five millimeters in diameter, surrounded by a barely visible erosive ring," the specialist said. "I note some trauma to the mucus membrane of the palate. Around the wound, there is a contusion zone, certainly caused by the gun being shoved into the mouth."

"So force was used?" Vidal asked.

"One could easily conjecture that the victim hesitated before pulling the trigger and thrust the gun against the roof of the mouth in a final act of determination," Vilars said.

The observations raised even more questions.

The doctors returned to the autopsy, examining a bone splinter on the scalp. Extracting the splinter, they uncovered a bullet. It had cut through the dura mater.

"As you certainly know, death from a .22-caliber bullet is generally the result of the direct gunshot to a vital organ, rather than the ballistic pressure wave, also known as hydrostatic shock. The .22 is commonplace but also one of the least effective kinds of ammunition available," the ballistics specialist explained.

Vilars used an oscillating saw to remove the skullcap. A strong odor wafted through the room, and Nico held his breath for a few seconds. Thirteen days after death, even in cold storage, the brain had collapsed. Despite the latex injection done at the university, Vilars noted the signs of subdural hemorrhage, which was the cause of death. Then she removed the brain and the cerebellum for dissection.

"The wound is clean, consistent with a .22-caliber bullet."

"From the trajectory, it is clear that the bullet was shot from the front, upward and to the left," Vilars specified.

"I assume that explains the cracks on the incisors," Nico said.

"Yes, it does," Vilars answered. "However, we cannot confirm that the victim broke his teeth on the weapon, although it does seem highly likely. In any case, the bullet trajectory would lead us to believe that if this was a suicide, Bruno Guedj was right-handed."

The detectives looked at each other. This was something they needed to check.

Vilars dropped the bullet into an evidence bag. "You can take this to the forensics lab. Now let's continue."

The two doctors carefully dissected the jaw in silence. After a while, Vidal began shifting from foot to foot.

"Don't be impatient, Captain," Vilars said. "If the teeth were damaged when they came into contact with the gun, it could have been self-inflicted. As with the contusion on the palate, he could have forced the gun into his mouth and bitten on it in a final show of resolve. At any rate, we'll have to do a tox screen. Did the university keep blood and tissue samples? I believe that is part of the protocol."

"Yes, they did," Nico said.

"I recommend that you requisition the samples."

The two police officers remained silent while the rest of the body was examined. Vilars described each part of the procedure in detail. They found nothing definitive suggesting a homicide. Bruno Guedj had no ligature marks on his wrists or ankles. There were no other indications that he might have tried to defend himself. The only troubling elements were the dental fractures and the wound in the roof of his mouth. And those factors, combined with the message found in the tooth, were enough to make Nico doubt that it was suicide. Nico suspected that Armelle Vilars shared his suspicions.

The autopsy ended shortly before lunch, but the chief medical examiner was not finished. An accident had occurred on the outskirts of Paris, and she had to confirm the identity of the victims, establish the causes of death, and determine who or what was responsible.

A happy surprise awaited Nico in his office on the Quai des Orfèvres. Caroline was standing at the window, looking out at the Seine. Seeing her made Nico forget all the questions surrounding the Bruno Guedj investigation.

"I didn't come to debauch you," she said. "I suppose you have tons of work."

She had brought sandwiches and sodas.

"Good idea. Eating can't hurt," Nico said.

"Anything new in the molar mystery?" she asked.

"Nothing for now, but we've just started our investigation. All I can say for sure is that I'm having a hard time believing it was suicide. I think that our man felt like he was in danger, and the message in his tooth was his only option."

"You'd have to be really desperate to come up with a plan like that. And the message could have gone unnoticed, even if he did donate his body to medical science."

Nico finished up his sandwich and pulled her close.

She ran her fingers through his hair and pulled on it gently.

"I left a message for the precinct chief in the seven-teenth arrondissement this morning," Nico said. "He's a friend."

Before disappearing, Sylvie had lived near the Parc Monceau.

"I'm sure he'll call back," Caroline said, pulling away. She picked up her things and got ready to leave.

"Be careful. The sidewalks are slippery," he said, adjusting her coat collar.

"Oh, by the way, I've arranged for a few days off between Christmas and New Year's, as we planned."

"You've got months to make up for, considering all that overtime you put in!"

"That's the pot calling the kettle black."

"Get out of here, before I eat you alive."

Caroline closed the door behind her, and Nico breathed in her lingering scent, as if to capture it forever.

He barely had time to sit down again before someone knocked on the door. It was David Kriven and the rest of his squad. Claire Le Marec and Jean-Marie Rost followed them in. They had spent the morning working on the molar mystery.

"Let's start with the police report," Nico said.

Kriven jumped in. "To sum up, on November 20, at 3:32 in the afternoon, Mrs. Guedj called the paramedics. She had come home and found her husband slumped over his desk. Dr. Philippe Owen arrived with the first responders and pronounced Bruno Guedj dead. He informed the police, who then did a quick investigation. They discovered a semiautomatic lying at his feet. There were traces of gunpowder residue on his hand. Tests done on Mrs. Guedj showed none. A detail: she didn't know that her husband owned a gun."

"Which hand had the residue?" Nico asked.

"The right."

"Professor Vilars told us that Guedj had to be right-handed if this were a suicide," Vidal said.

For the time being, nothing contradicted the conclusion reached by the local police officers.

"In addition, Guedj left a letter for the family saying that he was at the end of his rope, and he was sorry," Kriven said.

"We need to send that letter to the lab to check for prints and compare the writing," Deputy Chief Le Marec said.

"I'll take care of that as soon as we've finished here," Kriven responded.

"The officers had also found antidepressants in the bathroom. Mrs. Guedj said that her husband had been on edge for several weeks, but he hadn't told her why. The couple had two sons, ages sixteen and twenty. Bruno Guedj was a pharmacist who owned a drugstore on the Rue Thiron in the fourth arrondissement."

"You'll have to go there and question the staff," Nico said. "What about the semiautomatic?"

"It was a Unique DES 69, which falls into the fourth category of civil firearms and requires a license. Guedj should have gone to the local police station for the license, but he didn't."

"There is a flourishing black market," Rost said.

"Perhaps, but was Guedj really the kind of man who would buy a weapon that way?" Le Marec asked.

"He was depressed and apparently suicidal," Rost said. "In cases like that, a person will do anything."

"True enough," Nico said. "What about ammunition?"

"They didn't find any in the home and deduced that he had no intention of missing the target," Kriven said.

"That's strange. What's become of the gun?"

"The local authorities followed procedure and sent a request for destruction to the Police Weapons and Explosives Department on the Rue des Morillons in the fifteenth arrondissement."

Gunsmiths authorized by the department to destroy firearms kept logbooks and sent dated and signed receipts to police headquarters. The law did not impose any time limits, so they could reasonably hope that the gun was still in one piece. Only thirteen days had passed since Guedj's death.

"I'll get my hands on it and figure out where it came from," Kriven said.

"Remember that Guedj could have bitten into the barrel and cracked his teeth in the process," Pierre Vidal said. "It would be interesting to have the lab examine it. I already dropped the bullet off."

"Perfect. That's all for the local police investigation. What about Dr. Philippe Owen?" Nico asked.

Captain Frank Plassard, the second-ranking detective in Kriven's squad, spoke up. "I went to see him. He said everything pointed to suicide. Case closed. He signed the death and noncontagion certificates for the body donation. Mrs. Guedj was aware of the arrangements her husband had made and wanted them respected. Dr. Owen said the whole idea disgusted him, but he had to respect the man's wishes. He gave Mrs. Guedj a sedative and advised her to see her doctor to deal with the stress of losing a loved one."

"Owen didn't have any doubts?" Rost asked.

"None at all. For him, it was a classic suicide scene. Mrs. Guedj's attitude fit that of a tearful widow in the midst of—let's see, what were his exact words?" Plassard pulled out his notebook and flipped through the pages. "There it is. Dr. Owen's description: 'in the midst of psychogenic shock caused by overwhelming emotional factors.'"

"Amen," Kriven said.

"The rescue center will get us the recording of Mrs. Guedj's call."

"What's forensics saying?" Nico said.

Lieutenant Almeida responded. "Professor Queneau first examined what the message was written on."

Charles Queneau headed the police forensics lab. He was a kind of Professor Calculus, the character from *The Adventures of Tintin*, but stronger and more endearing. He had become distant from his colleagues since losing his wife a year earlier. Nico could understand. He couldn't imagine losing Caroline. Just the thought made his heart race. There were too many things that could rip a loved one away.

"It's transparent polyvinyl chloride, otherwise known as PVC, a widely used plastic. One example is the plastic used to protect the covers of bound documents. This piece was two micrometers thick. Scissors were used to cut it out of a sheet of plastic that you can find in stores anywhere and online. It's impossible to find the source. The message was written with a fine-tipped permanent marker, which is just as commonplace. Professor Queneau also found traces of what is most likely Guedj's saliva. He will be comparing that with the DNA samples we provided. The plastic had no prints or trace evidence."

"That will have to do, then. Can the lab confirm that Guedj wrote the message hidden in his tooth?" Nico asked.

"They called in Marc Walberg," Almeida said. Walberg was the lab's top handwriting expert.

"Let's get Guedj's good-bye letter to him, and tell Queneau I'll be at the lab in an hour," Nico ordered.

The phone rang. Nico picked it up and exchanged a few words with the caller. He ended the call and turned to his team. "That was Michel Cohen. He wants us to meet at six thirty. A run-through for tomorrow's sting. You're to be there, Jean-Marie, along with Théron and Hureau."

"I can't wait until we're done with this jewel heist," Rost said.

"Then you can get back to giving your son his bottle, and your wife will be able to get some sleep," Kriven said.

"Our good prefect will also be able to sleep better," Nico said. "That said, don't forget that our credibility is on the line. Pierre, can you summarize the autopsy results for our friend here?"

Captain Vidal did as he was told.

Then Nico turned to Le Marec. "Claire, I'd like you to call Mrs. Guedj and explain the situation. Can you do that?"

"Of course. I suppose I should tell her as little as possible."

"It's best not to say anything about the message for the moment. Tell her that we'll stop by and see her tomorrow at around eleven."

They all stared at Nico, who guessed what they were thinking. It was a shady case, but did the head of the Criminal Investigation Division really need to show up in person at the widow's house? He had enough to do elsewhere.

Kriven dared to break the silence. "Given that this story will be told fifty or a hundred years from now, you want to be a part of it, right? You want to see your name in the textbooks?"

"In the headlines and all?" Vidal said.

"And with any luck, it will be ten times bigger than any other," Kriven joined in.

The others applauded.

"Laugh all you want, but I get the feeling that this case hasn't finished surprising us," Nico shot back.

Deputy Chief Rost nodded. "I agree with you. It smells fishy."

Homicide was something of a team sport. Nico savored the solidarity and group spirit. A cell phone rang just as everyone was standing up to leave. Almeida pulled out his phone and glanced at the screen. He put it on speakerphone.

"Lieutenant Almeida, is that you? It's Queneau here. I've got something for you on the Bruno Guedj case. It's strange. You see, we've come up with this theory over here, if you've got a few minutes to spare."

7

The police forensics lab was at 3 Quai de l'Horloge on the Île de la Cité. The street owed its name to the clock, or *horloge*, that towered over the Paris courthouse complex, the Palais de Justice. Running along the Seine between the Pont au Change and the Pont Neuf, it seemed to channel a north wind, and in the old days it was called the "street of the dejected." Dejected was what Nico and Pierre Vidal were feeling at that moment.

Walking briskly from 36 Quai des Orfèvres and going through building security took exactly four minutes. The lab occupied four floors and some temporary structures in the courtyard. The place was pieced together and not at all suited to its use. Furthermore, some of the departments were in other areas of Paris. Professor Queneau had been waiting for the lab operations to be consolidated in a new building for so many years, he no longer believed it would happen. He had confessed this to Nico. Now he was a few months away from his retirement, and he no longer believed in miracles.

Nico knew that Queneau wasn't looking forward to his retirement. Since losing his wife, he hated holidays and didn't take all the vacation time he was entitled to. He spent little time with his daughters and grandchildren, giving the excuse that he had work to do. The lab, which brought together a number of disciplines and top-notch experts, was the only place where he could forget about everything, and especially about the cancer that was eating away at him. Cancer had an advantage over the criminals, whose pursuit both he and Nico were dedicated to. Unlike the criminals, who wound up arrested and convicted, the disease seemed to go unpunished.

"Welcome to our modest home. It's always a pleasure, Chief," Queneau said, greeting Nico.

"The pleasure is mutual," Nico responded. He loved this part of an investigation, driven by technology and advances in criminology. Yet Nico believed that nothing would ever replace a detective's science of deduction and ability to see the big picture.

"Follow me," the head of the lab said, leading them into the room used to examine documents. A few people in white coats looked up from their work in a near-military-style greeting. Marc Walberg was the only one not to react, although Nico noted an involuntary twitch in his left eye. Walberg was pathologically shy.

"Please sit down," Professor Queneau said, waving to the chairs in front of two computer screens. He typed, and the message found inside the victim's tooth appeared on one screen. The official body donation letter appeared on the other screen. "Marc?"

Walberg took a deep breath. "To begin, let me remind you that forensic document analysis allows us to authenticate documents and determine whether they were written by the same person. We study four aspects of the writing. We start with the form of the letters, which includes their slant, their size, how close together they are, and any specific markers, such as whether the writer used 'and' or an ampersand, and how he or she dotted his or her i's. After that, we look at the content. Then we identify any tics in punctuation, grammar, spelling, vocabulary, and formulation. The quality of the lines and how it's all arranged are the other criteria."

Professor Queneau interrupted. "Despite easy access to printers, we have found that most criminals write their notes by hand. It's a sin of pride."

"In this particular case, the comparison is difficult," Walberg said. "The message is succinct and written in pen on a very small plastic surface. Furthermore, neither document was written spontaneously. The wording was thought out, and the writing was done slowly and methodically, which makes it hard for a graphologist. Because of this, I focused on the author's brushstroke. For example, whether it was consistent or disguised. People follow strict patterns from childhood when they write. These patterns influence how they hold the pen, form the letters, and space out words and lines. The brain is programmed for repetitive tasks and habits. From them, it is possible to sketch someone's personality."

"So?" Nico said, always patient with Walberg.

"He had quite handsome handwriting. That shows a good, most likely traditional education, one that was strict and required legible penmanship. From the form of the letters, one can deduce a desire to please."

"Were you able to confirm if the writer was a man or woman?" Vidal asked.

"Times have changed so much, Captain. We need to avoid sexist stereotypes. Women have no problems demonstrating their leadership qualities, just as men no longer hide their sensitivity. That said, women do tend to put less pressure on the tip of the writing instrument and have more rounded letters. It would seem to me that a man wrote this letter, but I say that with a margin of error of about twenty-five percent."

Nico and Professor Queneau glanced at each other. They knew the man. Walberg was careful by nature, and they could reduce that margin of error by at least fifteen points.

"This is where it becomes interesting," Queneau said.

Walberg nodded and pointed to the screen. "You see these smudges? They tell us that the writer was left-handed."

"How do the smudges indicate that?" Nico said.

"Marc is saying that the man who wrote these twisted his wrist clockwise to write from above. The man was left-handed. There's no question. When you dropped off the bullet, didn't you mention that the shooter was probably right-handed?"

"In the suicide theory, yes."

"Then that theory is incompatible with our findings, sirs."

Nico's suspicions that the suicide was staged were being confirmed. And the person who carried out the hoax had made a mistake. A serious mistake.

"There is this other letter, which the victim is thought to have written to his family before committing suicide," Vidal said.

Professor Queneau removed the sheet of paper from the evidence bag, handling it with care. He examined it for a long moment under a microscope and used several lights to uncover any other trace evidence or prints.

"It's iridescent ivory-colored paper made by Clairefontaine. You can buy it anywhere, including online." The growth of online shopping meant that cops no longer went from store to store to follow leads as often as they had in the past. Criminals had unlimited buying options at stores that weren't brick and mortar.

The professor continued. "The ink is standard quality. The pen tip produced a line of average thickness. With this electrostatic detection device, we'll look for impressions. If something were under the paper while he was writing, we might be able to pick it up."

He clicked, and a pharmacy cross, the familiar emblem of French drugstores, appeared at the bottom of the page, along with part of an address.

"'Pharmacy, Rue Thiron.' It's from letterhead," Nico said.

"There are several sets of prints on the document. I will at least be able to determine if any of them belong to our victim."

"Go ahead," Vidal said. "There will be those belonging to the police officers, the doctor who was called in, and the victim's wife."

"I will see to it," the professor said. He stepped aside so that Marc Walberg could examine the paper. The handwriting specialist furrowed his brow and pushed his glasses up his thin nose. Nico knew that this particular expression meant "do not disturb." Walberg imposed ritual silence whenever he worked, and it applied to everyone except Charles Queneau.

"The letters have the same shape, and the writing is similar. Left-handed, again. As with the previous samples, I'd say that it's not spontaneous. It shows signs of tension and stress, more so than in the body donation letter."

Nico and the others considered what Walberg had told them. "Good work," Nico finally said.

"You'll get the specifics in our report," Professor Queneau said. "The fluids found on the piece of plastic are being compared with samples taken from the victim. I suspect the news of the day is Bruno Guedj's lateralization."

"Yes, it is news that he's left-handed," Nico said.

Nicole Monthalet punched the speakerphone button to include all three people in the conversation. It was better that the police prefect hear about Bruno Guedj's strange death from her, rather than through the grapevine. Nico was in her office to provide any details the boss asked for. All three agreed that the next day's raid to nail the jewel thieves would occupy the media, distracting them just enough to keep the molar mystery out of the news if there were any leaks.

After talking with the prefect, Monthalet called the public prosecutor to inform him of the developments in the case.

Nico was well aware that Monthalet was always juggling these two authorities: her superiors in the police force—the police prefect and the minister of the interior—and the judiciary power represented by the public prosecutor, who answered to the minister of justice, and the independent investigating magistrates named to the cases. Nico rarely dealt with the prefect directly; that was reserved for Nicole Monthalet and Michel Cohen. But he worked closely with the justice system, following the criminal procedure code. Basically, judges monitored police activities to ensure that the law was respected. The police had a field advantage. The justice system worked from case files, which made it hard for them to verify what was actually going on. At any rate, how well the entire system worked depended in large part on the relationships between the people in place and their faith in the various branches of government. And one did not become chief of the Paris Criminal Investigation Division without following the letter of the law. Nico was careful to do so.

In the end, the prosecutor encouraged Nico to continue his preliminary investigation. His detectives would need to show some criminal wrongdoing before they could open a full-on investigation and name an investigating magistrate. Otherwise, they would have to close the case.

When Nico returned to his office, Captain Franck Plassard was waiting for him. Like a referee flashing a red penalty card, he whipped out a USB key. "Here's Mrs. Guedj's emergency call. I think you'll want to hear this."

Nico plugged the flash drive into his computer to listen to the recording. This kind of call was considered public record and couldn't be destroyed. Sometimes it was used as evidence in medical malpractice lawsuits.

"Emergency Response Center. How can I help you?"

"My husband," a woman screamed. "It's my husband. It's bad."

"Calm down, ma'am. What arrondissement are you in?"

"In the third. The Marais."

"Okay, what's your address?"

"Ten Rue Roger Verlomme." The woman was sobbing. "Dear God, please come quickly."

"Calm down, ma'am. Do you live in an apartment?"

"Yes, yes."

"What floor?"

Nico visualized the operator inputting the information on her computer as she went along.

"It's the top floor, the fifth floor."

"Okay. Is there an access code?"

"One-one-four-A."

"What's the apartment number?"

"Fifty-one."

"Is your husband conscious?"

"No! He won't answer," the hysterical woman cried out.

"Is he breathing?"

"He's not moving at all. I don't think so."

"What is your husband's name, ma'am?"

"Bruno Guedj."

"Okay, how old is he?"

"Forty-seven. He's in his chair, and he's not moving!"

"Calm down. Someone will be there to help. I'm going to connect you with the doctor right away. Stay on the line, ma'am."

Part of the operator's job was screening calls to separate medical emergencies from other critical situations. Most medical calls were handed over to a competent specialist, either a hospital practitioner or an on-call doctor. In cases involving the ingestion of a toxic substance, the caller was connected to the poison-control center.

After a few moments of silence, the operator could be heard again.

"Ma'am, I have the emergency-response doctor on the line. He'll take over from here.

Nico heard a new voice.

"Ma'am, what exactly is happening?"

"He's not moving. Something happened to him!"

"Is he your husband?"

"Yes."

"Can he talk to you, ma'am?"

"No. He's not responding."

"Is he breathing normally?"

"I don't think so. Oh, my God!"

"Calm down, ma'am. We're here to help now. Are his eyes open?"

"No."

"If you ask him to open his eyes, does he try?"

"Bruno! Bruno! Open your eyes. Please, my love, please. Answer me!"

"Is he reacting at all?" the doctor asked.

"No!"

"Has he had any health problems recently?"

"No, not really."

"What exactly do you mean, ma'am?"

"He's been tired and stressed for some time now. But that's all."

"Where is he right now?"

"Sitting at his desk."

"Is he bleeding anywhere?"

"From his nose. Oh God!" Mrs. Guedj let out a scream. "There's a gun on the floor!"

"Ma'am, don't touch anything. A medical team is on the way, okay? They will take care of your husband. Did you hear me, ma'am?"

Nico had heard enough. He looked at Plassard.

"The doctor sent out a team immediately—an ambulance with an anesthesiologist and an emergency physician, Dr. Philippe Owen," Plassard said. "You know the rest."

"You can never be sure from a recording, but she seems genuinely upset," Nico said.

"That's my feeling, as well."

"She mentioned that her husband had been depressed recently, but she didn't seem to think he would commit suicide."

"As many times as I've listened to tapes like these, it always feels strange," Plassard said. "It's like you're right there when everything is unfolding. That poor woman."

"We have quite a few questions to answer," Nico said. "And the key one concerns that message in the tooth."

Someone opened his office door. "Sorry to interrupt," Michel Cohen said. The apology was a formality. Nico knew Cohen had something pressing on his mind that couldn't wait. "Nico, I'd like to see you before the six-thirty meeting."

Plassard cleared out. It was six twenty.

"Next week, Commander Hureau will be promoted to deputy chief and move over to vice," said Cohen, who had worked in the unit earlier in his career and was thoroughly familiar with its operations.

He moved on to the more urgent matter on his mind.

"There'd better not be any slipups tomorrow night," Cohen said.

"We've gone over everything," Nico said. "And don't pressure Hureau. He knows what he's got to do. He's a good cop, and tomorrow night won't change that. He's got the bit between his teeth. He deserves this promotion."

"I know, but we're all on edge."

By "all," he meant the commissioner, the prefect, the investigating magistrates, and the interior minister.

"Speaking of teeth, Nicole told me that you've sunk yours into a good one. She gave me the rundown on the case. What's your take on it?"

"It's strange."

"No kidding. It's the first time I've ever heard of a message being buried in a dead man's molar, and I've been around the block a few times. What's your gut feeling on this, really?"

"There's something shady about the whole thing."

"So you don't think it's a suicide?"

"I'm having a hard time with that. Bruno Guedj seems to have been left-handed, which we will be verifying very soon. But the gun was fired by someone who was right-handed."

"They found gunshot residue on his right hand, is that correct?"

Cohen had clearly read the case file.

"That's correct."

"Could someone have helped him—or forced him—to hold the weapon?"

"Why not? Perhaps the culprit didn't know that Guedj was left-handed."

"That's quite an oversight," Cohen said. "You know what I like about this work? Cops are smarter than all those shits! That's how justice prevails. Okay, let's go."

Nico got up and left the office with Cohen, closing the door behind them. He thought about Commander Charlotte Maurin, who would most likely be transferred from the Juvenile Division to take Hureau's place as squad leader. A good choice.

8

Nico never tired of Paris neighborhoods, which were like small villages, each filled with charm and legend. Walking the city, he often recalled something novelist George Sand had written: "I know of no city where ambulatory musing is more pleasant than here." The Marais was one of those exceptional places where time seemed to stand still. One could get lost wandering its main thoroughfares and narrow streets lined with mansions or slipping into the royal splendor of the Place des Vosges. The Marais had deteriorated over the centuries, until the nineteen sixties, when most of the buildings were restored, thanks in large part to André Malraux, who made it one of the first designated historical sites in the capital. Nico loved window-shopping, hand in hand with Caroline, along the Rue des Francs-Bourgeois. But more than anything else, he enjoyed hanging out in the art galleries with pink and white façades under the arcades on the Place des Vosges. He was drawn to the contemporary works of Fifax, Bouteiller, and Fazzino.

Now when he wandered through the Marais, would a vision of Bruno Guedj slumped in his armchair come to mind? Would he recall the decapitated head with a message hidden in its tooth? He knew that he would, although he—and the city—had seen many other crimes.

Nico and Claire Le Marec parked in front of 10 Rue Roger Verlomme. They rarely had the opportunity to work together, as they usually divided their tasks, but these moments built stronger bonds and helped them present a unified leadership.

Nico studied the blue double doors, which were now open. The Rue Roger Verlomme was parallel with the Rue Francs Bourgeois and crossed the Rue de Béarn and the Rue des Tournelles. From where he stood, the road widened. A nursery school, a church mission, and a bistro called Chez Janou were nearby.

Nico and Le Marec entered the building. It was Friday, December 4, exactly two weeks after Bruno Guedj had left the building for the last time, feet first.

The Rue Thiron was wide but short, lined with trees and perpendicular to the Rue de Rivoli and the Rue François Miron. The former was known the world over, but who knew that the latter was where King Louis XIV, the Sun King, had lost his innocence to a lady-in-waiting nicknamed One-Eyed Kate? Kriven and Plassard did. They had found out thirty minutes earlier, thanks to Nico Sirsky. In France, the casual study of history often yielded such little gems of information.

The green pharmacy cross stood alongside signs for a tobacco store and a newspaper and magazine shop. A bank, luxury stores, and a pastry shop were across the street. Kriven's stomach was grumbling.

"It's not lunchtime yet," Plassard teased. "It's not good to eat between meals."

"I'm not the one who hides cookies in his desk."

"A crime scene is like a boat on the high seas. It's better to go out on an empty stomach so you don't get sick," Plassard said, pushing open the door to the drugstore, which was filled with tasteful displays.

Claire Le Marec and Nico found themselves in a covered cobblestone passageway. A gate stood between it and the courtyard. Forty or so mailboxes filled one wall.

Under a pane of glass was a list of apartment numbers and residents, along with an old advertisement for SOS Chimneysweep. A metal touchpad on a stainless-steel plaque was embedded in the façade. Nico tapped in the code Mrs. Guedj had given him.

"Open sesame," he said.

The gate opened. The courtyard, surrounded on all sides by the condominium complex, was magnificent. A bronze statue of a cherub-like child with a cloth tied around his waist was in the middle of the space. He was holding a large vase above his head. It was filled with snow now, but Nico imagined that the vase overflowed with plants when the weather was warm. The ground-floor apartments had greenhouses. Nico looked up and counted five stories. The victim's apartment was on the top floor. Several doors led to different wings in the complex.

"There is a second entry from the street," Le Marec said.

They crossed the cobblestone courtyard and walked out on the other side, finding themselves at 5 Rue des Minimes. It was like some sort of magic trick. They went into the building and took the stairs to the apartment.

Nico rang the doorbell.

A woman who appeared to be about fifty years old greeted Kriven and Plassard at the counter. The badge on the lapel of her white coat read "Melanie, pharmacist." When Kriven showed his badge, the woman's eyes widened. She gulped and pursed her lips. Kriven asked to speak to her manager. A man in dark pants and a striped sweater came out from the back. Kriven guessed that he was in his thirties. He looked self-assured and even slightly pretentious.

"Could we go someplace quiet to talk?" Kriven said. His tone was polite but firm. "It's about Bruno Guedj."

The expression on the man's face changed instantly. Kriven tried to read him. Was it surprise? Apprehension? Relief? It seemed to be a mix of emotions, and that got the detective's attention. He looked at Plassard and saw that his partner was having the same reaction.

"Let's go into my office."

Mrs. Guedj was a pretty and curvaceous woman of forty-five with blond highlights in her hair. But her pale complexion and the deep purple circles under her eyes betrayed fatigue and stress. A young man who looked protective appeared behind her. Nico guessed he was the elder son.

"Ma'am, I'm Chief of Police Nico Sirsky, head of the Criminal Investigation Division. This is Deputy Chief Claire Le Marec."

"Please come in. This is my son."

Nico held out his hand to the young man, who followed them into a comfortable and tastefully decorated living room. Nico noted that there was a balcony, an incredible luxury in Paris. A thin coat of snow covered the garden furniture and bushes along the railing.

"As I understand it, you are questioning my husband's suicide," Mrs. Guedj said.

"The doctors at the Paris Descartes University made a strange discovery," Nico said.

Stoic, Mrs. Guedj waited for the rest.

"Your husband had a message hidden in one of his teeth, under a filling," Le Marec said.

There was another silence. Nico let Mrs. Guedj take in the information.

"Do you know who could have helped him do that? Perhaps his regular dentist?" Nico asked.

"Dr. Maxime Robert. His office is in on the Rue du Temple, next to the Church of Sainte Élisabeth," Mrs. Guedj answered. The pitch of her voice had risen.

"Did your husband have an appointment recently?"

"At the end of October. He got that horrible filling. He said it was just temporary."

"Had he complained of a toothache?"

Nico gave Mrs. Guedj time to think. "No, I don't think so," she said after a few moments. "I don't remember anything. It's odd, now that you mention it."

"I'm Denis Roy," the pharmacy manager said. "We were all upset by Bruno's death. It was so unexpected."

"Suicide is hard to predict," Commander David Kriven said. "But there are often changes in behavior in the weeks or months beforehand. It doesn't happen without a reason. Nobody here noticed anything?"

Roy sighed and looked away.

"Something is bothering you, isn't it?" Kriven said.

"I don't really know. He had changed."

"Since when?"

"September. He had become nervous. Actually, he looked tortured, nearly paranoid. He jumped every time the phone rang. He would look at people funny, especially if they weren't regular customers. He seemed to be expecting—or afraid of—something."

"Like what?"

"I have no idea."

"And you didn't ask him?"

"Yes, I tried. Melanie did too. He said it was something personal, nothing serious."

"Did you believe him?"

Denis Roy shrugged.

"He would get calls on his cell phone and either go talk in private or hang up. He'd be very distracted after every call. Something was definitely worrying him. And once, at the end of September, some weird guy showed up here."

"Had you seen the man before?" Kriven asked.

"Absolutely not. Nobody here knew him."

"Could you help us do a composite image of him?"

"Of course."

"What happened when this guy came in?"

"Bruno took him into his office and locked the door. There was some shouting, and the man left."

"And then?"

"Bruno clammed up. He looked afraid. He'd refuse to answer our questions about it."

"But you said your boss's behavior had changed before that meeting."

"That's right. It just got worse after the man came in."

"Which would explain why he bought a gun for the store," Plassard said.

"A gun? Certainly not. None of us here would own a firearm, despite the risks of the job. A pharmacy not far from here was robbed for uppers, but that didn't change our position on having a gun at this pharmacy."

"Are you sure?"

"If you're talking about the gun he used to kill himself, it didn't come from here."

"A Unique semiautomatic," Plassard said. "Are you certain that you didn't see it here at any time?"

"I'm not familiar with guns, but if there was anything even resembling a gun in this store, I would have known about it."

"Didn't Mr. Guedj have a safe?" Kriven asked.

"Yes, Melanie and I have the combination. We keep the day's earnings in it."

"Did you know that your boss was taking an antidepressant?" Plassard asked, pushing for information.

"No, I didn't." The pharmacy manager looked at the floor. "I should have known. Is that what you're trying to say?"

His pretention-tainted self-assurance was cracking.

"Not at all," Plassard said. "Clearly, Bruno Guedj wanted to tell you as little as possible. We are trying to understand why."

"What was on it? On the message?" Bruno Guedj's son asked, looking Nico in the eye.

"It won't be easy to hear."

"I want to know, and so does my mother."

"'I was murdered.' That's what your father wrote."

"Are you sure it was him?" Mrs. Guedj asked.

"A handwriting analysis confirmed it, and other tests are being done. Would you be able to provide us with anything that he wrote out by hand? That would help."

Mrs. Guedj stood up and left the room.

"My father hadn't really been himself lately. I couldn't get him to tell me why. I should have insisted."

"You're not to blame. Something happened, and he didn't tell you anything about it. He must have had his reasons. Maybe he wanted to protect you. It's our job to figure out what occurred."

Mrs. Guedj returned. "Our Christmas list. One evening at the beginning of September, we talked about buying presents for the holidays. You know how it is. Every year, we always start too late and end up shopping at the last minute. Then we swear that we'll do it differently the next time. This year we intended to stick with our plan. That night, we shared a good bottle of wine and made out the list. Bruno took everything down."

Taking the list from her, Nico glanced at her son. He seemed to be barely controlling his pain and anger.

"Did your husband have store letterhead here?" Le Marec asked.

"Yes, in his office."

"Can we have a sample, please?"

"I can find it," the young man said, getting out of his chair.

"The day your husband died, you told the police that he wasn't doing so well and was taking antidepressants," Nico said.

Mrs. Guedj was barely holding back her tears. "That's right. I still don't understand what could have happened. We had a good life, with our family and work. We were lucky. I loved my husband, and I believe he loved me. The children were doing well and brought us all the joy parents could dream of. I have no idea why Bruno suddenly became so sullen and distant. He refused to talk about it."

"You don't have any idea at all?" Le Marec asked.

"Believe me, I've wracked my brain, but I can't find any logical explanation."

"Did he have a prescription for the antidepressants? Was he seeing a physician?"

"No, he helped himself at the pharmacy."

Her son came back into the room and handed Le Marec the letterhead.

"When did his behavior begin to change?" Nico asked.

"In September."

"Not long after that evening when you talked about Christmas?"

"Two or three weeks later."

"Do you remember the date you made the list?"

"It was the weekend before our youngest went back to school, so it must have been on September 5."

"Which means something happened sometime between September 19 and September 26," Nico said.

"Yes, that's it. Bruno had a few phone calls that annoyed him, but that's all that I noticed."

"Who were they from?"

"He said it was work, and I shouldn't worry."

"What telephone did the calls come in on?"

"His cell."

"Did you overhear anything he said?"

"No, he locked himself in his office and then came out all agitated."

"You also told the police that you didn't know he had a gun."

"Bruno hated firearms. He would never have had one in the house, if for no other reason than to keep the kids safe."

"Did you tell the police that?"

"Yes, but still, it looked like a suicide. And Bruno left a letter asking us to forgive him. If he really wanted to end his life, it's easy enough to get a gun on the streets."

"Who told you that it's easy to buy a gun on the street?" Nico said.

"The officers who were here. It's frightening."

"Except that he wrote 'I was murdered' on a piece of plastic that he hid in his tooth!" her son shouted.

"Did he tell you about his decision to donate his body to science?" Commander Kriven asked.

"No, he didn't," Denis Roy said. "When we learned about it, we were all shocked—there was no funeral or anything. But Bruno loved his job and helping the sick. In the end, it's understandable that he would want his body to be put to good use."

"What's going to happen to the pharmacy?" Captain Plassard asked.

"I wanted to go into business for myself. Bruno knew it and was encouraging me. I had already started looking for a pharmacy. Then he died, and since there is no successor, the possibility of buying this business has come up. I met with the staff, and I'd like to stay here."

Kriven held his gaze. Guedj's suicide had come at just the right time for this manager.

"I just wish it hadn't happened this way," Roy added, fidgeting.

"Did Mr. Guedj make any provisions in the event of his death?" Kriven asked.

"Bruno was always planning ahead. He had life insurance."

"Was it a good policy?"

"Indeed. It was enough to provide for the heirs. The beneficiaries will get the money from the life insurance and the proceeds from the sale of the pharmacy."

Franck Plassard steered Roy to another topic. "He had paper supplies for the pharmacy, didn't he?"

"Yes, enough for day-to-day business."

"And sheets of plastic?"

"Maybe. I mean no. Nobody uses it for anything."

"What about Mr. Guedj's office?"

"We haven't touched anything in there. It's still too hard."

"Can we take a look?"

"Of course, it's right over here."

"Could the message have been some practical joke your father was playing?" Nico suggested.

"That's impossible," the young man cried out. "He would never do anything so childish. It's too…too hurtful. He wasn't like that. He would never have wanted us to suffer."

"What he says is true," Mrs. Guedj said. "Bruno would never have pulled that kind of stunt."

"On the day he died, you let Dr. Owen know that your husband had given his body to science," Nico said.

"Bruno made me promise. I wasn't keen on the idea, but I didn't have the strength to oppose him."

"You didn't agree with his decision?"

"It was so sudden. We never even talked about it at length. He just told me what I needed to do. He usually didn't handle things that way. Let's just say I felt backed against a wall."

"When did he tell you about his decision?"

"At the end of October. He gave me the papers and showed me where he kept his donor card."

"Did he tell you why he wanted to donate his body?"

Mrs. Guedj sighed. "He just begged me to respect his wishes. It was really important to him. Urgent, even. I didn't have a choice."

Le Marec looked at Mrs. Guedj's son. "You didn't know anything about it, did you?"

"No, I didn't."

"What's happening with the pharmacy?" Nico asked.

"Bruno made sure we'd be taken care of. And one of his employees, Denis Roy, offered to buy the shop. That's what my husband would have wanted."

"How did your husband make sure you'd be taken care of?"

"He did the usual things, like taking out life insurance. I'll have enough money for our children's education, and I won't have to sell the apartment, at least not right away. He arranged everything with our notary, who's handling the estate."

"And who is that?"

"Maître Belin."

Mrs. Guedj looked at her son. "His card is on your father's desk. Would you please go get it for us?"

"I'm no specialist in inheritance taxes and the like," she said after her son had left the room. "It's best that you contact Maître Belin. I'll let him know, so that he can give you what you need. He has handled our affairs for years. I'd be so relieved if you could help me understand what happened to Bruno."

"We will do our best," Nico said, speaking softly. "Did your husband have any other family?"

"His parents, two older sisters, an elderly uncle, and a second cousin he treated like a brother. Everyone got along well. Bruno's mother is in the hospital right now. She's getting on, and his death was a terrible shock."

"One more question. Was your husband right- or left-handed?"

"Left-handed."

Captain Franck Plassard searched Bruno Guedj's desk as his squad leader and Denis Roy looked on. Plassard knew what he was looking for.

"I found it," he said, pulling out a pack of transparent plastic sheets.

"We'll be taking this," Kriven told Roy.

"Why?"

"Routine verification."

Kriven looked around for anything in the office that would give him a better understanding of who Bruno Guedj was and what was eating at him. His eyes stopped on a picture frame. He walked over to it and examined what was inside. He read and reread the words, as if they couldn't be true.

Nico's cell phone rang. He stood up as he answered and headed toward the sliding door. Once he was on the snow-covered balcony, he closed the door behind him. He signaled to Le Marec to keep Mrs. Guedj occupied and stepped over to the railing and set a hand on the icy edge.

"I'm listening," he said, looking over the side of the balcony.

"Are you sitting down?"

"Better than that. I'm freezing my ass off on a balcony five floors up. Be quick, before I turn into a snowman."

"Aren't you Russians like huskies? Great trackers and resistant to arctic cold?"

"You got that right. I'm a great hunter and I love to work with my pack—as long as they don't bust my balls. Now get on with it."

"Okay, here it is: Bruno Guedj got his degree at Paris Descartes University."

Nico contemplated two seagulls fighting over a piece of bread. Central and Northern European birds wintering in a Western European city.

"You've got to admit that it's unbelievable, giving your body to your own school." Kriven was excited—Nico could hear it. "Returning to his past. What do you think it means?"

The seagulls flew off. Nico would have gladly followed them. He had dreams of traveling.

"He trusted them. He knew how things worked at the school, and he was betting that they would find his message."

9

One of the three antiterrorism squads had an office on the fifth floor, at the end of the hallway. Nico said a few words to the team members and then went back down the hall. A green sign with white lettering read "Bike Room." He grabbed the key from a box on the wall and opened the door. The ceiling was so low, he had to stoop. He climbed a set of metal stairs and finally reached the evidence room, which bore the nickname *séchoir*, or dryer. It was a tiny white-tiled room that was kept at the same humidity level and temperature year-round to safeguard the items stored here. Nico knew all too well that some people might consider the evidence room a horror museum. It had housed many bizarre and stomach-turning pieces of evidence.

Inside, five wooden steps led to a window. He turned the handle and entered a world to which only a privileged few had access. It was the rooftop of the police headquarters, which gave a breathtaking view of Paris. Here, Nico always had the feeling that he was overlooking the world. It was as close to Olympus as a common mortal could get, and he held the city and its famed monuments in his hands: Notre Dame, the Panthéon, Montparnasse, the Eiffel Tower, the Louvre, and, in the distance, the futuristic buildings of La Défense. The Seine, with its boats ferrying tourists to various sights, and the bridges and streets filled with cars and pedestrians were a divine urban labyrinth, a gift from the gods requiring no Ariadne thread.

Nico often came to this place to relax, even on a day like this, when the sky was gray and low, nearly threatening. Wrapped in his coat, he was thinking about Bruno Guedj. The evidence pointed to suicide. He had been depressed since September. The good-bye letter had his prints on it. The gun was at his feet, and there was gunshot residue on his hand. But it was on his right hand. That detail was enough to make Nico think that someone else was involved, someone who had harassed Guedj on the phone and perhaps had visited him at the pharmacy at the end of September. The police now had a sketch of the man, but it didn't match anyone on record.

Feeling threatened, Guedj had formulated a unique plan to disclose what really happened to him. The plan had two parts. In mid-October, he signed the forms to give his body to the Paris Descartes University, his alma mater, and at the end of the month, he asked his dentist friend, Dr. Maxime Robert, to help him hide a message under a rough filling. The plastic had only Guedj's DNA on it. Furthermore, the sheet of plastic and the pen used to write the message matched those found in the pharmacy.

All these measures seemed to be justified, because on November 20, Guedj had died from a gunshot to the head. Where did the gun and the bullet come from? Kriven was on that, helped by Professor Queneau's ballistics team. In addition, toxicology had turned in its report. They hadn't found any illicit drugs or medication in the samples from the victim. It was possible that Guedj had bitten down on the gun and cracked his teeth in a final defensive reflex.

Marc Walberg's handwriting analysis was more intriguing: The victim's good-bye letter showed signs of intense stress and apprehension. Was this the mind-set of a man a few minutes away from committing suicide or that of a man forced to write something before being murdered?

Nico and his detectives had this information, but it wasn't nearly enough. First, they needed more on the semiautomatic that was used and the bullet, which had been identified as a .22-caliber long-rifle bullet. Despite its name, it was common handgun ammunition. With any luck, they would find some trace evidence, prints, or some other element that would lead to someone who was already in the system. They also needed to look into the calls the victim received and Denis Roy's acquisition of the pharmacy. Was that a motive for murder? They would meet with Maître Belin and Dr. Robert and try to establish Bruno Guedj's schedule.

Nico heard a voice behind him. "You're going to turn into an icicle."

Deputy Chief Jean-Marie Rost had guessed where Nico was hiding. Like the other cops at headquarters, he used the rooftop for an occasional escape from the demands of the job.

"It's about time," Rost said. "The team is ready."

Nico stepped down from his aerie. It was nearly the end of the afternoon. Dusk would fall soon, and the officers from the division were all focused on the night's operation: locking up the Avenue Montaigne burglars.

The two men returned to Nico's office and were joined by Le Marec and commanders Théron and Hureau.

"We've fine-tuned everything," Nico said. "The bastards don't suspect a thing. They'll be behind bars before they have time to react." Nico turned to Hureau. "Make the most of your last night with La Crim'. You'll miss us soon enough."

"Starting Monday, you'll be living it up in the city's cabarets and dives," Rost joked. "Your wife must be thrilled that you've been transferred to vice. Or maybe you haven't told her."

"I told her that as a section chief, I'd end up just like you: stuck in the office with my ass in a chair. Easy and no danger."

"Smart-ass."

Claire Le Marec put an end to the banter. "Boys, your conversation is brilliant and all, but…"

Nico, Le Marec, and Rost were to meet at operation headquarters, while Théron and Hureau would head out to the field, armed and in bulletproof vests.

"It's time," Nico said, choosing to believe they would all come back in one piece.

10

The end was near. Like this snow-covered city spread at his feet. This city, pinned beneath a dark gray sky. At that moment, he wanted to pick it up and squeeze the buildings and crush the crowds. He would spread his hate and anger, making the world pay for his suffering. Yes, he was suffering. Even the powerful could suffer. But he would not surrender. There were no limits to what he was capable of. It didn't matter how many people died, how much blood flowed. He would have his way. Or he would have his vengeance. Even God, that bastard who was waving Christmas under his nose, could not stop him.

The end was near. But he still had time.

11

The room was dark. Nico slid under the sheets and nestled against Caroline. She purred. Her touch warmed him, and he began caressing her soft skin. He rested his hand just above her hip for a moment, and the stillness kindled his hunger. He pulled her closer. She turned, and they kissed, first softly and then more intensely. Nico ran his tongue down her neck and shoulder, pausing at her breasts to fondle her nipples. He heard her moan. He caressed her stomach and moved down to her thighs, finally reaching the place where he could give her the exquisite pleasure she anticipated. Her moaning grew more urgent, until she invited him to enter her. He obeyed. His desire was almost agony. Then there was only the bliss, the well-being that he could find in no country or city on this earth. Caroline's body, which he held in his arms, was his world. It was a world in which he delighted in getting lost, a world in which he found himself, over and over. It was ultimate and perfect.

The ringing pulled him from his sleep. He opened his eyes and saw that the sun had risen and was filtering through the curtains. Caroline turned over. He reached out and grabbed his phone from the bedside table.

"Nico?"

He sat up when he recognized the voice. It was Michel Cohen's.

"Did I wake you? Damn, you managed to get some shut-eye after the night we just had?"

What the man didn't say was that it was Saturday. Nico had gotten home at four in the morning and fallen asleep two hours later. His alarm clock read eight thirty. It had been a short night.

"I wanted to congratulate you, and the prefect will do so personally. You did excellent work. The thieves are behind bars, and the eighty-five million euros in jewels are where they belong."

"The organized crime team should get the credit."

"I won't forget them, but I know the work you did on this case, including all the meetings you held in your hospital room. And the interrogation you led after you brought them in will go down in the books."

The burglars had been handcuffed and taken to head-quarters. The Quai des Orfèvres had even been cordoned off to facilitate the transfer from the vehicles to the build-ing. Once they were inside, Nico had been responsible for getting one of them to talk. It had been trying. The man was filled with cold rage and refused to cooperate, but after an hour of questioning and subtle strategy, Nico prevailed. He walked away with vital information that led them to the loot. The division had delivered a KO punch, and the prefect had saved his job.

"That will keep the media busy over the weekend. They're already milling in front of headquarters. The prefect and Nicole will hold a joint press conference this morning. They'll mention you by name, and if you're lucky, we'll be seeing that handsome mug of yours on TV, too."

"Fantastic." Nico liked to see the police get the credit they deserved, but he preferred staying off-camera. Being recognized on the street made his job harder.

"You're not jumping with joy?" his bossed teased.

"You're quite mistaken. My team has been under pres-sure, and now they'll be able to breathe easier. We are all happy that you, Commissioner Monthalet, and the prefect can tell the press what we've managed pull off."

"Now I have to tell you to get your ass to the office. Get dressed, and be there at ten."

"Excuse me?"

"You heard me, Nico. I want you to be at the press conference with your counterpart from organized crime. The reporters are asking for you. You'll be finished by lunch."

"I'll be there," Nico said.

"See you later," Cohen said. He ended the call.

"What's happening?" Caroline asked, sounding sleepy.

"I have to go."

Caroline started nibbling his ear.

"Shoot. Jacqueline and André are picking Dimitri up at eleven."

"Don't worry," she said. "I'll explain. You'll be back when they bring him home." She was a doctor whose work hours often changed at a moment's notice. She understood.

"Can we have lunch together?" Nico asked.

"Yes, my love, we'll have lunch together."

Nico forced himself out of bed. Caroline followed him under the shower, answering his unspoken request. They played for a while with the soap and hot water, giggling like teenagers. Then he put on a suit and tie, while Caroline looked on.

"Will you kiss the sleeping prince for me?"

"If you mean Dimitri, he was up studying last night while you were out playing cops and robbers. He had some math homework to do."

"I suppose he took advantage of your expertise."

"Don't go thinking I hand him the answers on a platter."

"Oh, I trust you totally, Professor."

"Get out of here. You'll be late."

They kissed at the door. Then Nico took off for headquarters.

Bruce Springsteen's baritone voice filled the car. The streets passed by to the rhythm of "Dancing in the Dark." Nico could almost see the Boss strumming his guitar outside the car, his boots covered with snow. How did that man come by such talent? Nico's favorite Springsteen song, "Secret Garden," had always made him thirst for the sweetness of a love that had seemed elusive—a love that was "everything." Now he had that love.

Several reporters greeted him at headquarters. He climbed the stairs two by two, testing his physical condition. His leg still slowed him down a little, but he felt he could run a marathon. He presented himself to Nicole Monthalet's secretary.

"The commissioner is waiting for you," she said, smiling politely.

It was time to see the other boss. Nico put Bruce Springsteen out of his mind. He was all business as he walked into Monthalet's office.

Caroline set down her chopsticks after finishing the last piece of sushi. They both loved this unpretentious restaurant in front of the Palais Royal. The miso soup was delicious, the bluefin tuna was perfectly fresh, and the California rolls so big that Caroline had trouble fitting them in her mouth, which made them both laugh.

Hand in hand, they walked along the Avenue de l'Opéra, admiring the Palais Garnier and blending with the tourists before heading toward the department stores on the Boulevard Haussmann. This year, as fate would have it, marionettes and lights in the store windows celebrated Slavic culture and food. With childlike wonder, Caroline and Nico took in the displays at the Galeries Lafayette, where a brigade of animated pastry-chef bears was making a *bûche de Noël*. The Printemps windows held an imaginary trip along the Volga. Another showcase had been transformed into a dacha, where magical creatures played hide-and-seek with life-size Russian nesting dolls.

Reality and imagination seemed to blur. Where was he? Was he holding Caroline's hand on the Boulevard Haussmann, packed with holiday shoppers like a subway car at rush hour? Was that the smell of roasted chestnuts in the crisp winter air? Or was he part of this magical Russian scene, dancing with the woman he loved before pulling her behind a nesting doll to kiss her in secret?

Work life intruded. Did Bruno Guedj kill himself? Or was it cold-blooded murder? Was his death the act of a desperate man at the end of his rope? Or was he mixed up in some dirty business? Had he seen or heard something he shouldn't have? Had he made his murderer angry or afraid?

"Where are you?" Caroline whispered in his ear.

He started. "In Russia."

"In a charming little wooden chalet in the middle of the snow?"

"A fire in the fireplace, lying on a bearskin." He smiled.

"With me?"

"With you. Naked."

"Liar."

"What do you mean?"

"You weren't thinking about Russia anymore. Your eyebrows were all bunched up. So, are you going to tell me where you were?"

Nico sighed. She read him like an open book, and he was actually glad. "I was thinking about Bruno Guedj."

"Oh."

"I know. There's no connection to any of this, except that his suicide seems about as artificial as these dolls and landscapes. An illusion. Well, we have a meeting to go to," he said with a smile.

They walked briskly along the sidewalk, past the famous jewelers on the Place Vendôme—Mauboussin was Caroline's favorite. Finally, they reached the Rue de Rivoli and the tea salon Angelina, with its refined Belle Époque atmosphere. Anya was waiting for them.

Nico's mother was a tall, slender woman with hair that was still blond, thanks to her hairdresser's subterfuge. Her eyes were pale blue, and her bearing was proud. Men still turned to look at her when she passed. She had set her Russian rabbit-fur cap on the table. Anya loved to cultivate her roots, down to the smallest detail.

Her eyes brightened when she saw Nico, and she gave him a warm hug. Anya's gravelly voice always took Nico back to his childhood, when she would read to him: poems and novels by Griboyedov, Pouchkine, Lermontov, and Gogol. She read the pages with the talent of an actress, moving with ease from laughter to tears. That voice affected him profoundly. It felt like the voice of a forgotten heroine in an old black-and-white movie. But Anya herself was a colorful character in the pure Slavic tradition. She was a woman nobody forgot.

"You look superb, my dear," she said to Caroline.

Anya had taken to Caroline immediately. Nico knew that Anya thought his new love had all the necessary qualities to make him happy, unlike Sylvie. Anya had been civil to her daughter-in-law, but she considered Sylvie a bad mother and a horrible wife.

They ordered the tea salon's rich and delicious hot chocolate, along with three *monts-blancs*—meringue with chestnut puree and whipped-cream filling. Tourists the world over came to Angelina to sample this delicacy. The line of foreigners waiting to get into the tearoom was proof of that.

"So Dimitri is with his maternal grandparents?" Anya asked right away.

"Don't worry. It will all be fine," Caroline said. "I think they are very kind people, don't you?"

"That is true," Anya said. "And André is the only grandfather Dimitri has left."

That was what Nico had told his mother when he broke the news. Given Anya's feelings about Sylvie, he had expected her to vent about his former in-laws spending time with Dimitri.

"I have nothing against them at all," Anya said. "Just Sylvie."

"Nico told me that they never denied their daughter had problems. I understand they tried to help her."

"I can't say the contrary."

Nico's mother was hard to predict. She had so much bitterness against his ex-wife, this would have been a fine occasion to express it. But it was clear that she was relieved to see her son with someone she thought he deserved, and she never wanted to hurt Dimitri. Anya loved Dimitri as much—perhaps even more—than she loved Nico. So she had nothing mean-spirited to say about her ex-daughter-in-law today.

"You are a very perceptive woman, my dear," Anya said to Caroline. "I am happy you are here with us, at this table."

At the end of the afternoon, Jacqueline and André Canova rang the doorbell. When Nico opened the door, he saw the happiness on their faces, which were pink from the cold. They also looked older. He regretted not contacting them sooner. But didn't Caroline always say that things happened when they were meant to happen? They hugged Dimitri a final time before letting him go.

"It was really cool to see you again," Dimitri said. "Let's do it again soon, okay?"   Tall   and   well-built already, with deep-blue eyes and blond hair, Dimitri looked so much like his father. Nico was even more astonished at how much he and his son thought alike. Dimitri had the same sense of duty and responsibility. Nico had sometimes put his own aspirations aside because of that sense of duty and responsibility—to Sylvie, for example. Nico wanted Dimitri to pursue the dreams he had for himself. But helping him do that wouldn't necessarily be easy. Nico knew Dimitri took pride in being like his father.

"Caroline seems to be a fine woman," Jacqueline said. "Dimitri loves her. That's clear. We are happy for you, Nico."

"Thank you. But Sylvie needs to come back. That's what we're hoping for."

André began walking away without saying a word. Jacqueline gave Nico a worried look. He returned it with a reassuring nod. He was on it.

Nico closed the door. It had been an excellent day. Tomorrow, Sunday, he would spend time with his family. Squash with his son and Caroline, a new convert to the sport, then brunch with his sister, Tanya, her husband, and their children. They would take a walk in the afternoon and return home to read novels on the couch.

Then there was Bruno Guedj, a ghost to remind him that life was not always so sweet.

12

Notaries were professionals who never ceased to astonish Nico. Their role in the French legal system was well rooted in history. As early at the third century, civil servants in Gaul, then part of the Roman Empire, were authenticating documents. Notaries disappeared with the Barbarian invasions, only to be resuscitated by Charlemagne. From that point on, notaries grew in power under kings of France, including Louis IX the Saint, Philip IV the Fair, and Henry IV. Much later, in 1945, the Conseil Supérieur du Notariat was created by law. It had a large hand in rebuilding the country following the Second World War. After that, the notary's sphere of influence quickly expanded into many areas of French life.

Nico had a somewhat cynical view of notaries. In his eyes, the notary was a relatively clever human capable of adapting to historical upheavals and finally becoming an indispensable administrative cog in everyone's life, from marriage to death. In biology, that kind of living organism was called a parasite, because it fed, found shelter, and reproduced by establishing a lasting relationship with its host. But Nico had to give credit where it was due. There were some beneficial parasites that didn't necessarily damage the host—or, in this case, the client.

Nico had come across more than a few notaries in his life. They were all conscious of their image. They tried to give the impression that their clients' interests were even more important than their own. To do this, they used the most refined language, dressed conservatively, and acted like grade-school teachers. But put a few drinks in them, and they let their hair down. In the end, they were like everyone else, prisoners of their role. Wasn't that the case with the majority of jobs? Indeed, there was something fundamentally easy to caricature about notaries, which made Nico actually like them, despite his reservations.

Maître Belin didn't disappoint. Dressed to the nines and seated behind an antique oak and mahogany desk, he looked down on them. The chairs occupied by Nico and David Kriven were slightly lower than the notary's armchair. It was an old intimidation tactic. Rugs covered the hardwood floor, and an imposing bookshelf was filled with law manuals.

"I can confirm that Mr. Guedj wanted to see me to make sure that his affairs were in order."

"Did he do this often?" Nico asked.

"No, not really."

"What were his objectives?"

"To make certain that his family was protected in the case of some lapse on his part."

"By lapse, would you mean death?" Nico asked, not without a touch of sarcasm.

"That is correct. Mr. Guedj mentioned a friend who had died suddenly, leaving his family in an uncomfortable situation. He said that it had shocked him, and he would not have the same happen to his wife and children."

"When did this appointment occur?" Kriven interrupted.

"On Monday, October 19."

"What, exactly, did you talk about?"

"His life insurance. Mr. Guedj wanted to go over his coverage with me, as he feared that his policy would be null and void were he to commit suicide."

"And was that the case?"

"That particular restriction applied only during the first year of the policy. So he was covered in the case of suicide."

"How did he react to this news?" Nico asked.

"He seemed relieved."

"Didn't that surprise you?"

"Mr. Guedj did not seem to be a man who would take his own life, although he did seem to be more anxious than usual. In any case, the information was protected by notary-client privilege, and Mr. Guedj was sure to remind me of that."

"What else did he ask you to do?" Kriven asked.

The notary nodded, looking uncomfortable. "We also discussed his other insurance policies."

"And what were they for?" Kriven asked. Nico saw that Kriven was becoming annoyed, probably because getting straight information from the man was like pulling teeth.

"Those covering the mortgage on the pharmacy and the loan on his apartment on the Rue Roger Verlomme. There, too, suicide was covered."

"So, to sum up, Guedj's loans would all be covered if he were to commit suicide," Nico said. "In addition, he made sure his heirs would have money to cover their needs, thanks largely to the sale of the pharmacy."

"It does not qualify as a fortune, but Mrs. Guedj has no worries for the future, and her sons' educations will be paid for."

"Did you not find all of this somewhat curious?" Nico said, trying to imitate the notary's formality.

Maître Belin looked away.

Nico went on. "I venture to ask: are these not the actions of a man who is trying to put his affairs in order before committing the unthinkable?"

"I cannot answer that question," the notary said. He was becoming testy. "I repeat, Mr. Guedj seemed to hold his life dear. He appeared to love his wife and two sons deeply and not to have any desire to abandon them. Evidently, the events have proved me wrong."

"Have you told his widow about your meeting with him?" Kriven asked.

"No, it was privileged, as I said, except in your case. In addition, I had given my word."

"To Bruno Guedj?"

"He demanded it."

"And is that because he shared his concerns with you?"

Sweat beads appeared on Maître Belin's forehead. He took a breath and composed himself. "Of course I was worried. But Mr. Guedj was quick to quiet my concerns, reiterating his desire to see his sons become men, play with his grandchildren, and grow old with his wife. He added that there were no guarantees that he would be able to do those things. He could fall victim to some bad luck. Something unfortunate could happen to him. So he wanted to make provisions for his family. His declaration sounded like an epitaph, I admit. But I took him at his word."

"Which you asked for, in the same way he did," Nico said, not expecting an answer.

The notary stared at him. Touché.

Then Maître Belin's voice thickened with emotion. "Why did you come here to discuss all this?"

"He talked about some bad luck or something unfortunate happening, right? Were those his exact words?"

"That's what he said. I remember it perfectly."

"Thank you for your cooperation, Maître Belin."

Nico and Kriven stood up to leave.

"I remain at your disposal. Am I to deduce from your visit that you are looking into the possibility that Mr. Guedj did not commit suicide?"

"I expect you to keep that among us."

"Is it possible that you have discovered something?"

"It is possible that he did not commit suicide, Maître."

"Please keep me informed. His death was a shock to me, as you can imagine, and I would be relieved to know that it was not a suicide. I would feel that I helped to protect his family, instead of holding the weapon that killed him."

"In any case, you were not the one holding the weapon. If Bruno Guedj did kill himself, you bear no responsibility."

"Thank you," Belin said.

They left the quiet office and dived back into the hub-bub of the streets.

"Damn it, boss," Kriven let out as they walked to the car. "Did you learn to talk like that at Science-Po? If we'd been there any longer, you would have been calling him as 'my good man.'"

"Traditions, David. Traditions. French cultural expec-tations, good taste, and all that."

"Is that what you call it? I'd say mothballs. Paris pol-lution never smelled so good."

Just as they were getting into the car, Kriven's cell phone rang. It was his second-in-command, Captain Plassard. Kriven pressed the speakerphone button so Nico could hear.

"Vidal and I are just leaving Maxime Robert's place," Plassard said.

Church bells, those belonging to Sainte Élisabeth on the Rue du Temple, could be heard in the background.

"His friends call him Max. A jolly fellow, fiftyish, graying hair. But at the mention of Guedj, Coco the Clown turned pale. He immediately made time in his schedule and gave us half an hour. He seemed sincerely demoralized and glad to see us. He had lost all hope."

"What do you mean?"

"Guedj had scared the daylights out of him. But he had promised Guedj that he wouldn't tell anyone about his visit to the office at the end of October. Guedj had even said that their families' lives would be in danger if he opened his trap. Dr. Robert admitted that he had been having a hard time sleeping since his friend's death. He was praying that the cops would show up, because Guedj had said that only then could he spill the beans."

"What beans?"

"Guedj asked him to drill a hole in a healthy tooth, put a piece of plastic inside it, and cover it with a gross, ugly filling. There was nothing temporary about it. Guedj wanted to attract attention once he died."

"And Dr. Robert agreed to do this?"

"Yes, he went along with it."

"Did he read the message before putting it in the tooth?"

"Guedj categorically refused to let him, saying the dentist's safety was at stake."

"What drama! You said they were friends?"

"Their families didn't know each other, but the two of them went out for drinks on occasion. They had met for drinks in July, and Guedj was fine. When Max saw him at the office at the end of October, he was a changed man—extremely nervous, almost tormented. When Dr. Robert didn't hear from Guedj again, he called two or three times to check on him. Guedj never answered. Then he found out that Guedj was dead."

"And the dentist seemed to take his concerns seriously?"

"He had been hoping that Guedj was just going through a bad spell and perhaps imagining things. But our visit today seemed to confirm that there was good reason to be afraid."

"Why was that?"

"It proved that Guedj wasn't just being paranoid," Plassard said. "I had the distinct impression that Max was going to send his wife and kids out of town to stay with an old aunt with a house deep in the woods."

"I'll talk it over with the chief, but I don't see any-thing that would justify placing these folks under police protection," Kriven said. "Just in case, find out where the old aunt lives. Maybe we'll send word to the local police."

"Consider it done. Hugs."

"Yeah, right, I'll give you hugs you'll never forget."

Kriven ended the call, and Nico and he didn't say anything. Nico finally broke the silence.

"Two weeks ago—a simple suicide. Today—a mystery that's becoming more complex by the minute."

The day had been intense. Nico was multitasking, reviewing the various cases his detectives were investigating and going over terrorist threats related to the holidays. He would have to arrange for appropriate defensive measures. Although the lion's share of his job involved investigating and solving homicides, Nico handled the gamut of major crimes, from missing persons and kidnappings to those terrorist threats. Meanwhile, Kriven and his team were focused on Bruno Guedj. Seventeen days had passed since his faux suicide, which was a seventeen-day advantage for the culprits. Enough time for them to think they were safe, but not enough for them to escape the division's top sleuths. Nico felt sure of that.

He looked from Rost to Kriven, who were sitting in front of him. They had made progress, positively identifying the firearm and the ammunition that caused Guedj's death. The ballistics report had come in from the police forensics lab. Would it support Nico's suspicions or not?

"David requisitioned the gun, which had not been destroyed," Rost began.

"The serial number didn't give us crap," Kriven said, sounding irritated. "The weapon is not on state records. It *doesn't exist.*"

"The DES 69 is one of the best competition handguns, still used, even if it is no longer being produced," Rost said. "Shooting clubs have tons of them. Gun laws have changed since the nineteen seventies, but that kind of firearm could be handed down in a family without any-one realizing that it needed to be registered. It's in high demand on the black market."

"Forensics looked for fingerprints and trace evidence. They took it all apart. Nada."

"Bad luck, but foreseeable," Nico said.

Kriven went on. "As for the .22-caliber long-rifle bul-let pulled from the skull, it's standard. It's a widespread and frequently used bullet. The lab guys shot the DES 69 and compared the bullet they used with the bullet found in Guedj's skull. The trace marks are identical. So they concluded that the gun was the one used to kill Guedj. Then they checked the database, hoping the gun had been used before, but again, nada."

Kriven was referring to the firearms database man-aged by the National Forensics Institute in Lyon.

"In any case, you can find .22-caliber long-rifle bullets everywhere—in any gun shop and online," Rost said.

"Mrs. Guedj insisted that her husband had never owned a gun," Nico reminded them. "Getting back to the question Claire asked, would he have been able to get one on the black market?"

"He really wasn't the kind of man who was used to black-market dealings," Rost said.

"No, he wasn't. It would have been much easier to take a bottle of pills, which he could just pull off a shelf."

"How ironic: a pharmacist with access to any number of potentially lethal drugs shooting himself in the head," Kriven said.

Nico went back to his questions. "And what about the theory that Guedj cracked his teeth biting down on the weapon?"

"There are, in effect, traces on the barrel," Rost confirmed. "Professor Vilars took imprints of the victim's teeth, and Plassard got his dental records from Dr. Robert. With all of that, the lab came up with a computer-generated three-dimensional bite print and simulated the teeth chomping down on the gun, and everything fits."

"Good work. That said, Guedj could have bitten down in either scenario—if he was killing himself or if someone was about to murder him." Nico reached for the phone. His secretary was calling to announce that Helen Vasnier and Bastien Gamby were there to see him. He almost sent them away before turning back to Rost and Kriven. "The antiterrorists are here to see me. Does this have anything to do with you?"

"You gave me the idea," Rost said.

"Send them in. Thank you."

Helen Vasnier led the antiterrorist investigation and training squad, and Bastien Gamby was her computer specialist. Both were top-notch agents who worked on a variety of investigations under Nico's orders.

Vasnier was fiftyish and looked like a professional from an old spy movie: severe bun, houndstooth jacket, and plain leather pumps. A short pearl necklace polished off the image. She was a timeless mother figure to everyone in the division, her skills deserving of their blind trust.

Bastien was an altogether different sort. With tousled hair and coloring as pale as a sheet, he lived in a parallel world—the world of the Internet. Dimitri would have called him a "no life." Bastien was capable of surfing the web for hours, even days, fueling up on nothing but chips and soda. With his eyes cemented to the screen and his agile fingers typing away, he weaved his way through networks of bastards and cybercriminals: identity thieves, forgers, con artists, stalkers, sexual deviants, and terrorists. He talked to his computer, as though it were his best friend.

"Deputy Chief Rost had us do a little something for you," Helen Vasnier said. "He asked us to identify a number found on Bruno Guedj's cell phone. If I understand correctly, Guedj was getting harassing phone calls before his death. The number you're interested in, which was used to contact Guedj between September 23 and November 16, appears to be suspicious. According to our research, it was used to call Guedj and no one else and has not been used since. In addition, the calls all came from relay antennas inside the city."

This was a significant piece of information. "Mrs. Guedj said her husband started acting depressed before that, in mid-September," Nico said. "How many calls were made from that number?"

"Seventy-eight calls in about eight weeks, which would mean that he was getting nearly ten calls a week," Vasnier answered.

"That would be enough to spook anyone," Kriven said.

"Digital technology and mobile phones are a gold mine for police surveillance, but the bad guys are having a great time with them too," Vasnier said. "Bastien?"

"Yes, Chief."

"Tell us about the number."

"It's a burner phone, not the throwaway kind, but one with a prepaid SIM card. The authorities may be fighting anonymity, but they are not there yet. In France, you're supposed to have some ID to get a prepaid SIM card, but in Barbès you can get one pretty easily on the street. The store owners don't always ask for identification. Even the places that are stricter can be taken in by a forged ID. That's what happened here. It led to a fake name and address."

"Damn it," Nico let out.

13

Two days later, Nico received a call on his cell phone. He stared at the screen for a few seconds, worried that it was bad news. It was the precinct chief in the seventeenth arrondissement.

"I know where your ex-wife is," the man said.

Nico's shoulders relaxed. Sylvie was still alive. "Where?"

"At a seaside resort in Charente-Maritime."

"A seaside resort?"

"It's a resort with a treatment center for people with anxiety and depression. They help clients get off their meds, minimize their symptoms, sleep better, and so on. It's legit. Shrinks run the place. Your ex-wife is staying in a three-star residence on the grounds."

Sylvie had an aunt who lived in Royan, on the Atlantic seaboard.

"The center is in Saujon," the man continued.

That was in Val-du-Seudre, about fifteen minutes from Royan and fifteen miles from the Paris-Bordeaux highway.

"I can contact our guys there to double-check and even get her records, unless you prefer to handle that personally."

"I'll take care of it," Nico said.

"I'll send you the information by e-mail."

"Thank you."

"I know your plate is full at the division, with the holidays and all. It must be crazy there."

"The season's usual terrorist high alert."

"Hey, congratulations on rounding up those jewel thieves. Great work. I'm happy I could help you on this matter."

"You did help, believe me. It's a huge relief. Thanks again."

"No problem. Anytime."

So Sylvie had decided to get treatment. Good. It was the only way she could come back and be a good mother to Dimitri. As Nico took in the news, he heard a knock at the door. Jean-Marie Rost walked in, with a file under his arm.

"I have the preliminary report."

This was a key document in the investigation. It was prepared for the chief prosecutor, who would review the facts, establish a timeline, and draw conclusions. Nico skimmed through the pages, which he had already read and annotated.

"The die is cast," he said.

"The prosecutor will have to act on this," Rost said. "There are too many unanswered questions."

Half an hour later, Nico presented the report to his boss. Nicole Monthalet asked a number of pertinent questions and finally admitted that Bruno Guedj's suicide reeked of a setup.

Together, they went to the fourth floor, where there was a private door, used primarily by Monthalet and guarded by the division. It was an ordinary-looking door at the end of a hallway, and it led directly to the offices of the chief prosecutor. It was one of the secrets of the monolithic Palais de Justice and its two hundred thousand square feet of government administrative space.

The police commissioner knocked twice and then opened the door. She was greeted with the respect due her, given the position she held, and the prosecutor saw her immediately.

"A real case for the textbooks," he said. "Which side do you come down on, Commissioner? Suicide or murder?"

"I share the division's opinion. This is a murder."

"Tell me about it," the public prosecutor said as he started reading the file.

Nicole Monthalet explained the case, and Nico had little to add.

"The use of that cell phone with the burner SIM to harass Guedj is enough to call for an investigation," the prosecutor said. "Add to that the encounter with the stranger at the pharmacy and the fact that the victim supposedly pulled the trigger with his right hand, which makes no sense because he was left-handed. And then there's the message in the tooth. I think we can call this a homicide."

"That is our conclusion in the preliminary report," Monthalet said.

"We'll go ahead and open the investigation," the public prosecutor said. "I'll give it to Magistrate Becker. Any objections? Nico, I believe you and Becker make a good team."

Indeed, Nico and Becker had worked together. Nico hadn't cared for the man when he first met him. He seemed arrogant. But the two had gone after a serial killer together, and Nico had gotten to know the investigating magistrate much better. In fact, they had become close friends. Magistrate Becker would soon have full control of the investigation, much to Nico's liking. He couldn't wait to unravel it.

Nico walked across the Place Dauphine, nicknamed "the golden triangle" because of its geometry. André Breton, a founder of Surrealism, had likened the Place Dauphine to a female pubis. Nico preferred to think of it as the main haunt of detective Jules Maigret, the well-known fictional character created by Georges Simenon.

Curiously, despite the millions of visitors who came to the Île de la Cité to see the Notre Dame Cathedral, the Conciergerie, and the Palais de Justice, the Place Dauphine was spared much of the tourist traffic. Weather permitting, people played *pétanque* under the chestnut trees. Others walked their dogs, and lovers kissed on the benches, the very same benches Simone Signoret and Yves Montand had sat on decades earlier. The married actress and actor had lived in an apartment in one of the old townhouses lining the square. On this day, however, it was cold, and the square was deserted, with the exception of a few bundled-up regulars leaving nearby restaurants. Maigret had loved the *blanquette de veau* served at the Brasserie Dauphine. Simenon had based restaurants in his books on those in the neighborhood, including the tiny Taverne Henri-IV in the middle of the Pont Neuf. Nico had a late lunch date there.

He opened the door and asked for the table bearing the copper "Maigret" plaque. It was just the right spot. Maigret—the fictional head of his division, the Brigade Criminelle—had enjoyed his food and drink. And this restaurant, with its charcuterie, snails, tripe, and cheeses aged in the cellar on site, offered simple and satisfying cuisine.

A voice came out of nowhere. "Daydreaming, are you?" Magistrate Becker stood in front of him, a half smile on his face.

"Greetings, my friend," Nico said.

"Sorry I'm late. I finished reading the preliminary report. Now I understand why you've invited me to dine at Maigret's table. Maybe his spirit will help us. We'll need some intuition and insight to solve this one."

"What may I serve you, sirs?" a young man in a black apron asked.

"Two cheese and charcuterie plates, and, um, what's on the board," Nico said.

That day's wine recommendation was written on the blackboard in question-and-answer form. "What's the boss drinking this week? Château Ramage La Bâtisse, Haut Médoc, 2006."

The dining room was emptying, and soon they would be alone. Then they would be joined by those who came in after two to have a cup of coffee or nip of brandy.

"How is your wife?"

"As well as she was two weeks ago, when we all had dinner together," Alexandre Becker answered. "And since we're friends, I can tell you that Stephanie still kisses like she did when she was twenty. Isn't life beautiful?"

"You've got sex on the brain, Becker."

"Really, and you don't? Have you convinced Caroline to move in with you?"

"I'm working on it."

"It'll happen. Don't worry. By the way, have you heard anything from Sylvie?"

"She's hiding in a spa near Royan."

Becker looked him in the eye. "Have you told your son?"

"Not yet. I want to call her first."

"You're right. Test the waters before diving in. The current might pull you under."

Nico nodded at the comparison. The server brought their plates and glasses of red wine, and the two men dug into their gourmet picnic.

Still chewing, Becker got down to business. "So, Bruno Guedj didn't kill himself. QED. Next step: find out who was harassing him, who killed him, and why."

"Aye, aye, Captain," Nico said, swallowing a mouthful of Bordeaux.

"Any ideas?"

"You're leading the investigation now."

"What about starting with a search warrant for the victim's home and workplace?"

"You read my thoughts."

"We'll need to put together Guedj's schedule from September to the date of his alleged murder."

"I think we can tighten the time frame," Nico said. On September 5, Guedj had a romantic dinner with his wife, and all was well. Then, on September 23, he got the first anonymous phone call on his cell phone. His wife dates his behavior change between the nineteenth and the twenty-sixth. So something happened between the sixth and the twenty-third."

"Good thinking. What about that Denis Roy, the guy buying the pharmacy? Do you think that was motive enough?"

"We'll have to look into it. We don't want to neglect any lead."

"But you wouldn't bet on it?"

"Not a kopeck."

"I think you mean not a cent."

"A kopeck is good."

"You're going to end up emigrating, you know."

"I just want to see the country."

"You do know that they invented this thing called an airplane, don't you? Other than the search warrants, what do you suggest?"

"Questioning the neighbors, as usual, to see if any-one noticed or heard something unusual on Friday, November 20, the day Guedj died. We could show the composite image of the fellow who showed up at the pharmacy. You never know."

"Could a gunshot from a Unique semiautomatic go unnoticed?"

"It's possible."

"What do you think of the dentist and the notary?"

"I think we've gotten what we can from them," Nico said.

"That message in the tooth is odd. You need quite an imagination to think of doing something like that."

"Or you need to feel cornered to the point of giving your body to science and praying that a doctor will find it."

"It's completely crazy!"

"And Guedj gave his body to his alma mater, betting on the expertise of the faculty there," Nico said.

"This is the stuff horror movies are made of. He actually wrote the message, 'I was murdered.'"

"The man must have been terrified. Truly terrified."

Becker savored his last piece of cheese and ordered coffee.

"I'll get the warrants to you right away. Plan to search the two places at five this afternoon, if you can."

Nico and Kriven's squad arrived at the Guedj home. Detectives armed with the composite image began knocking on doors.

Nico found himself facing Mrs. Guedj, who was clearly exhausted. He presented her with the search warrant signed by the investigating magistrate. Her face crumbled.

"We are looking for evidence that could clarify what happened to your husband," Nico said.

Mrs. Guedj stepped aside to let them enter. "Will you search everywhere?"

Nico could see that she was shaken. To her, it had to seem like a violation. "We have to, ma'am. We'll be respectful." Nico was aware that most people had preconceived ideas about police searches. On television, the police spilled out drawers and tossed things all over the floor. In reality, that destroyed evidence and upset bystanders, neither of which real officers wanted to do.

"Dad didn't kill himself, did he?" the older son asked.

His brother was in the background, and he looked angry. This once-sheltered boy, having lost his father, was getting his first taste of life's injustice.

"We have reason to believe that might be the case, but we don't know for certain, which is why we are investigating."

"We want to know what happened," the boy said.

"We're on the same side," Nico responded.

"Thank you for trying to find out what happened to Bruno," Mrs. Guedj said, her voice sounding weak. "After all, you're not obliged to."

"Daddy had no reason to shoot himself in the head," the younger son cried out.

"Romain," his mother shouted, grabbing his arm. The boy calmed himself. There was an infinite sadness in his eyes.

Nico gave his team the signal to begin. Plassard and Almeida would search the main rooms, while Kriven and Vidal would head to the office. Nico asked the family to wait in the living room before joining them in the office. The detectives put on gloves and explored the shelves, the drawers, the credenza, and the desk, looking for anything that could have served as a hiding place. Kriven turned on the computer and ferreted through the files. Vidal inspected the man's papers, while Nico looked on.

"Guedj must have kept a calendar," the chief told Kriven and Vidal. "Let's find it."

A voice rang out from the other end of the apartment. "Chief!" Nico left the office and headed to the couple's bedroom. Plassard was holding up a notebook.

A telephone number was on the last page. The number had three question marks behind it and was underlined. Nico grabbed his phone and punched in the number. It rang several times. Then a female voice announced in a monotone, "This number is not in service."

Nico called Bastien Gamby. "Check to see if Guedj called this number, would you?"

"You got it, boss."

Nico dictated the number and ended the call. Then he returned to the office. Kriven was sitting in Guedj's armchair, a leather-bound personal organizer open in his lap. He gave Nico a thumbs-up. Nico recognized the number, written across the columns corresponding with Tuesday, September 15, through Sunday, September 20.

"Gamby's already on it," Nico said, just as his phone rang. "Speak of the devil."

"Guedj called it four times on Tuesday, September 15, and seven times between then and the following Sunday. That's all."

"At what time did he make the first call?"

"Four minutes past noon."

"Thanks, Bastien," Nico said, ending the call. "Who did he think he was calling? Where did he get the number? I want to know everything he did between September 6, the day after his tête-à-tête with his wife, and four minutes past noon on September 15, when he started making those phone calls. Find out where he ate, who he saw, where he took a piss—every detail."

"We're on it," Kriven said.

Nico left the room with the nagging feeling that they were missing something. In the living room, Mrs. Guedj was trying to soothe her younger son. His head was on her shoulder.

"Mrs. Guedj, you said earlier that your husband refused to tell you what was bothering him. You also said that this worried you, and you agonized over the cause of his change in behavior."

"That's correct. Where are you going with this?"

"You said you had no logical explanation for the change. Those were your exact words. Now think carefully, Mrs. Guedj. If I asked you what absurd, illogical thing that could have happened before everything changed, what would you say?"

14

At first, she didn't seem to understand the question. But then Nico saw that her pupils were dilated. She was thinking. Nico hoped she was digging through her memories, trying to uncover anything that could have provoked the bizarre chain of events. What could have convinced this man that he would be murdered? What made him so sure of it that he asked his dentist to hide the accusation in one of his teeth and arranged to have his body donated to science in the hope that someone would find that tiny piece of plastic? By all indications, he was a man who loved his family, a man who would not have abandoned them by committing suicide. And then there was the matter of the good-bye letter. It rang false. Even if he was depressed to the point of killing himself, Nico sensed that Guedj's words would have been gentler.

Nico read these thoughts in Mrs. Guedj's face. Then he saw a wave of anger sweep over her, a tidal wave capable of destroying everything in its path. She swallowed, and Nico thought he heard a crash in the silence. Mrs. Guedj stood up, her fists clenched. She seized a lamp and tore at the wire. The younger boy hid his face in his hands. The woman hurled the lamp against the wall, and it shattered in an explosion of glass shards. Kriven bounded into the room, a hand on his holstered gun. Plassard was on his heels.

"They killed Bruno," she screamed. "That's it, isn't it? But why? Why?"

"What did Bruno see? What happened to him?" Nico asked softly. No one moved. "Bruno came across something, didn't he, Mrs. Guedj. What was it?"

"Something crazy," she said.

"Something insignificant for you or me. Not necessarily ordinary, but insignificant. Something that became catastrophic for your husband."

The woman began to shake. "Bruno ran into an old acquaintance. It was stupid."

"Go on."

"A friend from school. They hadn't seen each other since then. Bruno seemed…well, surprised. And that friend gave him a fake phone number."

"Did he mention the man again?"

"No, not really. When I asked, Bruno said a lot of water had flowed under the bridge in twenty years, and if this man wasn't interested in renewing their friendship, that was his choice."

"So it didn't seem to trouble him that much?"

"I took him at his word. But then again, he did seem preoccupied. I figured that if his feelings were hurt a bit, he'd get over it."

"And was that the case?"

"I don't have any idea. I didn't bring it up again. Maybe I should have."

"It seems clear that your husband didn't want to mention it either, with all that water under the bridge, as he put it."

She looked down, the tension draining out of her.

"When did the encounter occur?" Nico asked.

She shook her head, unable to recall.

"Try to remember some point of reference. Was it a weekend, when the boys didn't have school? A weekday?"

Mrs. Guedj massaged her temples. Kriven and Plassard looked on wordlessly.

"It was a morning, sometime in mid-September. Romain was in school. Bruno had just come home from Vigot-Maloine."

"Is that the medical bookstore at the Odéon intersection?"

"That's right. On the Rue de l'École-de-Médecine. It's also a publishing house. Bruno was working on a book on drug compounding."

"Is that where he could have run into his old college friend?"

"It's possible. In any case, it was that morning."

"Did he have an appointment there?"

"Yes, with his editor. And Bruno loved to wander the aisles of the bookstore. The store was part of his life. Even when he was a student, he spent endless hours there. He had dreamed about being published by Vigot-Maloine."

"What time was his appointment?"

"Ten, I think."

"Your husband had the initials F.B. jotted down on his calendar, at ten on the fifteenth. Is that someone you know?" Kriven asked.

"François Brun is his editor."

"Bruno called the same number eleven times between the fifteenth and the twentieth," Nico said. "The number was not in service. That fits."

Mrs. Guedj and her sons looked at him, as if waiting for more.

"He called the first time on Tuesday at four past twelve."

"He came home for lunch that day, before returning to the pharmacy. He must have called before then."

"Okay. Do you have any idea who this old college friend was?"

"A med school student, I think."

"Did he mention a first name?"

"No. I admit it's strange. I expected him to tell me who it was, but he didn't. And I didn't press. It seemed that he wanted me to believe there wasn't anything to it."

Nico looked at his detectives. "We'll have to check his bank transactions and work out his schedule, particularly on that Tuesday, in the morning."

"I understand," Mrs. Guedj said.

"The quickest way for us to check his bank account would be online. Is that how you do your banking?"

"Yes, I manage our personal accounts online. Bruno took care of the big investments, such as the apartment and the pharmacy. We were planning to buy a vacation home in Brittany."

Nico gave her a compassionate smile and said, "Thank you for agreeing to review your checking account with the commander."

"What about my sons?"

"The only thing I ask all three of you is to keep this conversation to yourselves. Any of it getting out could compromise the investigation."

"You can count on us," Mrs. Guedj said, leaving the room with the boys. Kriven followed.

"Franck, give Jean-Marie a call," Nico said. "They should still be searching the pharmacy. Have him ask the staff if Guedj mentioned this old college friend or the wrong number. He called it eleven times. He was obsessed. How far would you have gone?"

"I would have broken down sooner and gone to see Bastien!"

"Not without my authorization."

"Of course, sir," Plassard said, cracking a smile.

"We need to follow this lead. It's the only one with any substance."

The captain nodded and stepped away to call Jean-Marie Rost. Nico decided to call Gamby. It was getting late, but Gamby never seemed to remember that he had a home. He lived at headquarters, in front of his computer. Gamby answered on the first ring.

"I figured you'd call."

"I want you to go through Guedj's phone records again. Here's the story. The guy runs into an old college friend he hasn't seen in twenty years. Said friend gives him a wrong number. For five days straight, he keeps trying to reach him at that number."

"That's stupid. It makes no sense."

"Exactly. After that, Guedj gets a series of anonymous calls between September 23 and November 16. The calls get to him, and he becomes depressed and afraid. He thinks someone is going to kill him, and he plans his counterattack."

"A posthumous counterattack."

"Again, exactly. He knows he can't escape the dark forces hounding him, and he is going to die. He tries something incredible, even impossible: taunting his murderers postmortem."

"It's the makings of a movie," Gamby said. His unflappable tone reminded Nico of the electronic devices Gamby worked with.

Gamby, like the other detectives at La Crim', was familiar with cases that blurred the line between fiction and reality. "What do you want me to look for?" he asked Nico.

"Other unusual calls, numbers he had never called before or gotten calls from, an increase in incoming or outgoing calls. Maybe he tried other means to reach his friend."

"What's the time frame?"

"From the day he ran into his former buddy, September 15, to the day he died in November. You'll have to compare that time period with previous months. Give Helen Vasnier a heads up."

Nico ended the call. The search of the apartment had been completed, and all the neighbors had been contacted.

"Nobody in the building heard anything the day Guedj died or recognized the composite image," Plassard said.

"The murderer must have had the code to get into the building, either 10 Rue Roger Verlomme or 5 Rue des Minimes," Nico said.

"Maybe Guedj had an appointment," Plassard said.

"An appointment with the murderer?" Vidal said. "Could he have given him the code? That seems crazy, doesn't it?"

"Yeah, but how else would the killer have known that Guedj was at home?" Plassard said. "Unless he followed him. How would he have gotten in, though?"

"Some good soul rang him in. It happens all the time. We may never know," Almeida said.

Plassard nodded. "That's possible. In that case, the man who came here was not the same one who visited the pharmacy, since no one recognized the image. A number of people could be involved in this thing."

"Let's say that's the case. They are probably careful and well organized. What did we get from the neighborhood canvass around the pharmacy?"

"Nothing more," Plassard said. "Rost got the list of customers who paid with a credit card or check on the day the unknown man showed up. Théron's squad has started contacting them. Two of the customers recognized the man when we showed them the composite. They described him as sinister-looking, dressed in black. He was the kind of man you notice, but he didn't seem to have much in the way of distinguishing marks."

"Did Guedj mention anything to his colleagues about meeting his old friend?"

"He told Melanie, who noticed that her boss seemed to be feeling a little dejected. She told him that most friendships last only so long, and many people don't want to renew ties with old buddies from the past. She advised him not to let it get to him. Guedj seemed to agree and never mentioned it again. Period."

Guedj's older son came into the room and looked at Nico. "Sir, they want you in the office."

The chief followed him to the office.

"On Tuesday, September 15, he made two purchases with his credit card," Kriven said. "The first at the book-store and the second at a pizzeria."

"He brought pizzas home for dinner," Mrs. Guedj said.

"It would be useful to know what time he made the bookstore purchase," Nico said.

"For that, we'll have to wait until tomorrow, because we'll need a warrant from Magistrate Becker," Kriven said.

"I think we've covered everything for today," Nico concluded.

The detectives said good-bye to the Guedj family, promising to keep them informed.

Outside, the harsh cold bit into their cheeks, but the city seemed unusually peaceful. The snow muffled the everyday urban noise. At the curbside, a father was pull-ing a Christmas tree from his car, reminding Nico that Caroline and Dimitri had talked about decorating the house the following weekend. Realizing that he would be with the two people he loved most in the world, while his ex-wife would be alone, three hundred miles away, he made a decision. He would contact her.

As he started his car and made his way into the stream of traffic, his thoughts returned to Bruno Guedj. He hadn't had the strength to fight. But in his despair, he had taken a wild gamble, sending a message from beyond in the hope that someone—some cop like Nico— would manage to follow the leads back in time to find the culprit.

Guedj had won the gamble. By the time Nico reached the Place de la Concorde, oblivious to the Champs-Élysées, which was festive with holiday lights, and the Christmas market stretched along the road to the Rond-Point, his resolve had strengthened.

That was when his phone rang. He answered, using his in-car speakerphone, and Bastien Gamby's voice filled the vehicle's interior. "I've got something."

Nico shivered. The noose was tightening.

"Guedj started making unusual calls on Thursday, September 17, which was two days after he met his old college friend. It went on for about ten days and then stopped."

The encounter at the pharmacy during the last part of September had probably put an end to his calls to that number. He knew there was something to fear. Unfortunately, it was too late. His fate had been sealed.

"Then he started calling the numbers he'd never contacted before," Gamby said.

"Yes…And what does that tell us?"

"I bet he was trying to be a master detective. Miss Scarlet killed Professor Plum with a knife in the conservatory. That kind of thing."

"Who, exactly, did he suspect?"

"One name stands out: Parize."

At that moment, Nico was sure they were headed in the right direction, and the wind was at their backs.

15

The dogs were out. How long before they came scratching at his door? How long did he have to get rid of all the evidence and keep up appearances? Damn it. He was losing ground. What good had all his success served? God was taking him for a ride. But the Almighty needed to hold on tight, because he intended to fight to the very end. He was a kamikaze. A killer.

16

The following morning, David Kriven walked into Nico's office without knocking. He waved a piece of paper at his boss.

"What's that?" Nico asked.

"Credit card records from the bank. Becker got us that warrant right away. Guedj bought something at the bookstore on September 15, at 11:47 in the morning. Seventeen minutes later, he called the number his so-called friend had given him."

"And the nightmare began."

"Jean-Marie is questioning Denis Roy."

"Perfect. We need to make sure that buying the pharmacy wasn't the motive for the murder."

Nobody was talking suicide anymore.

"My team is working on Guedj's schedule. Nothing of note yet, other than his appointments with the notary and the dentist. And we're going over all his calls again."

Who was the mysterious person Guedj had spoken to at the end of September? What did he want from him? Who was Parize?

"Any news from Claire?" Kriven asked.

An entire family had been killed in an apartment fire during the night. This kind of thing often seemed to have a relatively ordinary cause—malfunctioning heating equipment or careless smoking, for example. But in a number of cases, something criminal was involved. Claire Le Marec had a long day ahead of her with the explosive specialists from the crime lab.

"She's thinking it was arson. Are you ready?"

"Right behind you."

They were off to the bookstore. In the hallway, they ran into Dominique Kreiss, the division's only profiler. Deputy Commissioner Michel Cohen was skeptical about the role of psychology in police work, but he had hired Kreiss to stay current with the times. He didn't want to import American-style profiling to France, but instead to have a better knowledge of criminal psychology. She had turned out to be a priceless asset, particularly in her area of specialization: sexual offenses and murders. She worked hard and was determined to have her job recognized by the police officers and magistrates who remained distrustful.

"I'm working on a case with Hureau in vice," she said, stopping quickly to greet them. Then the shapely brunette with mischievous green eyes continued walking down the hall, with Kriven watching all the way. Nico punched him on the shoulder. Kriven held up his hands and gave a shrug of helplessness.

The Vigot-Maloine bookstore at the Odéon intersection was large and had a dozen or so employees. The atmosphere struck Nico immediately. Fascinated amateurs, students, and practitioners roamed the aisles full of books. An intoxicating smell of paper and glue hung in the air.

They showed their badges at one of the cash registers, and Bruno Guedj's editor materialized. The man's moustache seemed to complement his bow tie.

"I really liked Bruno and was shocked to hear about his death. I think about it often," he said, leading them up the stairs to his office, which was filled to the ceiling with piles of manuscripts. "Please sit down. We may not publish popular novels, but believe me, I receive submissions every day. Experts in every area want to leave something for posterity."

"Was Bruno Guedj one of them?" Nico asked.

"Yes. He was both a top professional and a fine teacher. His journal articles were remarkable. Unfortunately, he had not yet finished his book."

"It was about drug compounding. Is that correct?"

"Yes, that's it. One of his colleagues has agreed to finish the manuscript, and Bruno's name will appear first on the cover. All the royalties will go to his family. That is good news for his sons."

"I'm sure they will be touched by the gesture. According to his calendar, Bruno Guedj had an appointment with you on Tuesday, September 15, at ten in the morning."

"I checked my schedule while waiting for you, and, indeed, that was the last time I saw him. That wasn't supposed to be the case."

"What do you mean?"

"I'm not used to going two months without hearing from my authors. I tried to reach him and left three or four messages on his cell phone and as many at the pharmacy, but he didn't call back. I didn't want to bother his wife. At the same time, I wasn't especially concerned. Things always get more hectic toward the end of the year. I was planning to drive over to the pharmacy on the Rue Thiron if I didn't hear from him by the beginning of December. I regret that I didn't do it earlier."

"That probably wouldn't have changed anything."

"It's the 'probably' that bothers me."

"How did Bruno seem to you when you saw him on September 15?"

"Great. He was enthusiastic, happy to be alive, full of ideas. He even mentioned that he was thinking about teaching. I really couldn't believe he committed suicide. Just goes to show you: everything can change in just a matter of weeks. It's frightening."

"And then, after your appointment?"

"He browsed at the bookstore, which he loved to do. The bookstore has over thirty thousand titles, and you can easily spend a few hours looking through the shelves any time you visit. Bruno left with his arms full of books every time he came in."

"Did he talk to anyone that day?" Kriven asked.

"Everyone knew him. He'd been coming here for thirty years and was a good customer. I checked with Thibauld, the salesclerk who was working that morning."

"We would like to talk to him," Nico said.

They went back down to the ground floor and made their way around piles of papers, a photocopier, and a coffee machine that almost entirely blocked the hallway.

"Mr. Guedj asked for a book whose title he couldn't quite remember," Thibauld said. "I looked it up on the computer and went to find it on one of the shelves. He followed me. That's when I lost his attention. Literally. He just shut up and didn't say another word. He was staring at a man a few yards away. Then, after a few minutes, he went up to the guy. The man didn't seem to remember Mr. Guedj at first, but finally, he acknowledged him."

"Do you recall what he said?" Nico asked.

"He admitted that he was the man Mr. Guedj remembered, an old college friend. They hadn't seen each other for quite some time, and Mr. Guedj seemed excited."

"Did Guedj call him by name?"

"I'm pretty sure it was Christophe. That's my brother's name, which is why it stuck with me."

Nico silently thanked Thibauld's parents. "What was this Christophe like?"

"Ordinary. Mr. Guedj was excited about seeing him, but the guy didn't look like he felt the same way. He seemed very uptight, almost like a killjoy."

"What happened next?"

"Oh, it didn't last long. The guy said he had an appointment and left."

"How did they say good-bye?"

"Mr. Guedj insisted on exchanging phone numbers."

"And?"

"Christophe wrote down his number and took off. Generally, I don't intrude in the private matters of our customers, but Mr. Guedj seemed so thrown off, I wanted to say something to make him feel better."

"What exactly do you mean?"

"I told him that I ran into an old friend a while ago, and I realized that we no longer had anything in common. There was too much water under the bridge. Sometimes you just leave people behind."

Thibauld was some twenty or so years younger than Bruno Guedj, which didn't give him a lot of authority in the area of life experience. His words, however, had affected Guedj. He had gone home and told his wife that a lot of water had flowed under the bridge, and if his old buddy didn't want to renew an ancient friendship, it was his choice. But did he really believe that?

"I made up the story, of course," Thibauld said. "I just felt bad for him."

Nico smiled. He liked the young man.

"What did Mr. Guedj do after you spoke with him?" Commander Kriven asked.

"He paid for his books and left."

"Not long after meeting that Christophe, correct?"

"Fifteen or so minutes, no more."

Bruno Guedj had certainly tried to telephone the friend as soon as he left the bookstore. Why?

Kriven pulled out the picture of the unknown man from the pharmacy. "Is this the man?"

"No."

"Would you recognize Christophe if you saw him?"

"I think so."

"Could you help us come up with a picture like this one?"

"I'll try, of course."

Nico looked around the bookstore, with its thousands of books. He understood why Bruno Guedj liked it here.

Once outside, Kriven contacted Plassard. Rost had finished grilling Denis Roy. He was convinced that the manager was no killer and that buying the pharmacy wasn't sufficient motive for murder, especially because he was taking on a huge mortgage to do so. Nico was not surprised.

"What about Guedj's telephone calls?"

"The best for last," Plassard said. "Get back here right away, so we can tell you. It's big."

"How big?" Kriven asked.

"Sumo big."

"I don't know where you get your taste for suspense, Plassard," Nico said. "You'd better impress me, right now."

The Coquibus room smelled of testosterone. The team had been working nonstop.

"We called everybody Bruno Guedj contacted in the second half of September. Which member of the Parize family do you want, Chief? He called just about all of them. The mother, father, brother, cousins, and even the ex-wife. I wasn't joking when I said it was big."

Nico was getting impatient. "Where is this leading?"

"To a certain Christophe Parize."

"Christophe?" Kriven said. "Are you sure? That's the name of the dude Guedj saw in the bookstore."

"Positive. And Guedj didn't stop with the Parize family. He contacted friends they had in common back in their school days. And then he called colleagues of Christophe he didn't even know. Clearly, Guedj was investigating the man."

"Yes, it sounds like he wasn't just looking to hook up with an old college buddy."

"That's obvious, but there's something else," Plassard said. "There was a detail Bruno wasn't aware of. A big detail. Florence Parize, the mother, still hasn't gotten over her conversation with Guedj."

"Spit it out, Plassard!" Kriven shouted.

"Christophe Parize died last year, in early August. A car accident. He's dead and buried."

The room fell silent. Guedj had literally run into a ghost.

"But it doesn't seem that he took Florence Parize's word for it, because he kept on calling people," Plassard said.

"Tell me, at least, that he got the same answer every time," Kriven said.

"About that, yes. Everyone told him that Christophe Parize was six feet under. Guedj asked the mother, who knew him from his college days, to repeat it several times. When I mentioned that we were doing a routine inquiry into Guedj's suicide, I swear she nearly fainted on the phone. Before she hung up, she told me that she wasn't surprised. He had seemed upset."

"As far as our victim was concerned, Christophe Parize couldn't be dead," Nico said.

"That's what it looks like," Plassard said. "How could a man who died in a car accident more than a year ago be spotted in a store in the middle of Paris? Sure, nothing is impossible, but this has to be."

"Call Florence Parize again and ask her for a picture of her son," Kriven said. "I'll go back to the bookstore and show it around."

Plassard nodded.

"Kriven's on the right track," Nico said. "Start with the photo, and dig up everything you can about this Christophe Parize. Who is he, for God's sake?"

Near the second-floor stairwell, a door led directly to the central courthouse complex. Nico decided to use this access instead of the outside entrance, which required going through the snow. He found himself in a seemingly endless hallway with a high ceiling, bare white walls, closed doors, and uncomfortable, even hostile, benches. He passed several members of the Republican Guard, which, along with gendarmes from the provinces, was responsible for building security. Some fifteen thousand people came through the complex every day.

Nico finally reached Magistrate Becker's door and knocked. The magistrate's face relaxed at the sight of his friend. "So, what have you learned?"

"We're getting warmer," Nico said, recounting the latest developments.

"I see only one option," Becker said, shaking his head.

"I know what you're going to say."

"Do you have any other ideas?"

"No."

They fell silent for a few seconds. Then Becker let out a sigh.

"If the witnesses at the bookstore confirm that Bruno Guedj was talking to Christophe Parize, then I'll order an exhumation."

"I'll keep you posted," Nico said, turning to leave. He thought about Christophe Parize's family. The detectives would have to tell the family that the exhumation was part of a criminal investigation. It would be hard for them to take. And the prospect of dealing with yet another fragile family made him think of Sylvie. He couldn't continue to avoid her.

Nico took out his phone as he walked back to his office and called the Saujon resort and announced his rank. The receptionist transferred the call to the director.

"Sylvie Sirsky? There's no one here by that name," the director answered.

"Perhaps she's going by Sylvie Canova. That's her maiden name."

"Yes, Sylvie Canova is staying in a studio at our residence."

"When did she get there?"

"About a month ago."

"And how is she doing?"

"She had a rough start. Now I think she is doing rather well, all things considered."

"How long will she be there?"

"Several more weeks."

"Her parents and son are very worried about her. Is it possible to give her a message?"

"A few days ago, I would have said no, but she seems ready to resume some contact with her family. Her loved ones shouldn't expect any miracles. It will take time for her to return to everyday life."

"I'll let them know."

"You have my okay to call her directly."

Nico called Sylvie's parents immediately. The ball was in their court.

"How could André's sister have kept this from us?" Jacqueline said.

"Don't hold it against her. Sylvie must have demanded it."

"You're right. That sounds like our daughter. I can never thank you enough, Nico."

"I did it for Dimitri, too."

"You're a good father and a good man. It's too bad Sylvie didn't know how to keep you."

Nico called Dimitri next. His son was less enthusiastic about the news, having grown to distrust his mother.

Franck Plassard appeared at the door. "It's him. The bookseller recognized Parize in the picture. He's absolutely sure."

They were getting much warmer.

17

Despite the winter storm alerts for half of France, David Kriven and Franck Plassard left the capital at one in the afternoon on Friday. Chalon-sur-Saône in southern Burgundy was a little more than 130 miles from Paris. They could have taken the bullet train, but the weather was playing havoc with the schedule. So they drove—slowly. The roads were slippery, and they passed several cars in ditches along the way. A revised weather alert came over the radio as they pulled up to the curb and parked at the Place de Beaune. They had made it. Kriven turned off the engine. They left the warmth of the sedan. Everything was coated with snow, and the pedestrians looked more like trekkers than office workers on their way home.

"Shit." Plassard had just stepped in a puddle, soaking the bottom of his pants.

Kriven was wearing boots. "Always prepared," he said, pointing at them.

"Yeah, yeah."

"That café over there, Le Neptune, looks good," Kriven said.

Warm colors, plants, a large window overlooking the street, and comfortable seats welcomed them. French music from the nineteen eighties was playing in the background. Back then, the two officers were still in diapers. They ordered coffee and one of the wood-fired pizzas recommended by the owner, although it was still too early for dinner. As they waited to be served, Plassard studied the travel posters on the wall, which beckoned him with their faraway vistas and tanned vacationers. Even if he couldn't be in one of those places, this café was certainly more agreeable than the cemetery where they had an appointment.

They finished their meal. When it came time to pay up, Kriven asked how to get to the Western Cemetery on the Avenue Boucicaut. At seven thirty, Christophe Parize was to be exhumed by court order. This kind of operation in the nearly eight-acre cemetery was always done after closing hours and in the presence of a municipal police officer, who was responsible for making sure that all regulations were followed. Christophe Parize's body would then be transferred to the Paris medical examiner's facility. Alexandre Becker had ordered a genetic analysis to confirm the body's identity. In some criminal cases, proof could literally rise from the grave.

Outside, a kind of stillness reigned over the city, and the snow sparkled under the streetlamps. The two detectives walked past the courthouse and turned onto what had to be the most heavily trafficked street in the area, the Boulevard de la République. They walked under a bridge and turned onto the Avenue Boucicaut. They arrived at the entrance at 77 Avenue Boucicaut and presented the official documents. Kriven and Plassard were led to the Parize family tomb. By this time, Plassard was freezing.

Two stocky gravediggers with deeply lined faces were waiting for them. Getting the go-ahead to start, they used pickaxes and nail pullers to open the vault, saying nothing as they labored. Their faces quickly turned red from the cold and the effort, and clouds of condensation appeared with each breath they took.

"It's frozen," one said, his voice hoarse. He started coughing.

His colleague picked up a jackhammer. The din was nearly ear-splitting, and the pounding sent the snow flying. To Kriven, it looked like a swarm of insects shocked into action. Finally, the slab moved, and the gravediggers heaved up the coffin. The vault was made of concrete, which protected its contents from humidity and the gravediggers from biological hazards. That said, the arctic weather was their best ally, allowing them to work without safety boots, rubber gloves, and throwaway suits.

The two men set the coffin down with a final grimace. Was it from the exertion or the discomfort of desecrating a tomb? The detectives looked at each other, anxious to finish their task. The oak box was in good shape, and the gravediggers seemed relieved that they wouldn't have to transfer a rotting corpse to another container.

Two porters arrived to help put the coffin in the hearse. A strange funerary procession formed and weaved its way through the snow-covered forest of tombstones. One of the porters would take the body to the Paris coroner's office. Kriven imagined himself making the drive, focused on the rearview mirror the whole way, and he was glad that he wouldn't be the person behind the wheel of that hearse. He had visions of Parize sitting up, transformed into a bloodthirsty vampire or a zombie—sealed coffin notwithstanding.

They all said good-bye quickly, as if they wanted to forget this nighttime encounter in a deserted cemetery. Kriven and Plassard walked to their car and drove back to the entrance, where they joined the hearse. They would follow it to Paris and accompany the body into the red-brick building on the Quai de la Rapée.

Nico hung up. Kriven and Plassard had just gotten onto the highway and were headed toward Paris. Considering the weather, they would arrive at the medical examiner's office just a few hours before the autopsy, which was planned for the morning. Professor Armelle Vilars's work always spilled into the weekends, and she spent more time with the deceased than the living, especially her family. Had Nico been her husband, he would have set up a bedroom in one of the autopsy suites. Corpses could be trusted with lovers' secrets.

"So who is this Christophe Parize?" Police Commissioner Nicole Monthalet asked. She was sitting in his office, which she rarely visited. She looked tired.

"It's Dr. Parize. He was a hematologist who worked at Saint Louis Hospital. He was a practicing physician and full-time professor. He died in a car accident at the end of August last year at the age of forty-four. It happened while he was on vacation. He had been spending time with his parents at their home in Burgundy. He left two children and an ex-wife, whom he divorced not long before his death."

"I thought he went to school with Bruno Guedj. So he's not a pharmacist?"

"He has a degree from the Cochin-Port-Royal Medical School on the Rue du Faubourg-Saint-Jacques, next to the pharmacy school that Guedj attended. They did know each other at the time."

"Logically, the man couldn't be in two places at once, both dead and buried in a cemetery in Burgundy and alive in a bookstore in Paris. Professor Vilars will resolve that issue tomorrow. If the body is Christophe Parize, you'll be back at square one. And you may have to close the case if you don't have any other serious leads. Magistrate Becker will have to decide. But we're not there yet. I trust your instinct and judgment. It's true that the pieces fit perfectly—Guedj meets Parize, and the ball starts rolling. Those who fear that Bruno Guedj is onto something begin to panic. We're missing something, but we'll find it, won't we? Are you sure that Parize had no contact with his family after the accident? You never know."

"His parents are still grieving. His ex-wife seemed convinced that he is dead, and the children have not heard from him. Nothing from his colleagues, either. We'll have to dig deeper."

"Depending on Professor Vilars's conclusions."

Nico nodded.

"There was nothing to note before the accident?"

"A clearly difficult divorce is all that we've found."

"Fine. I recommend that you get some sleep, Chief. I hope you don't plan to get mile-by-mile updates from your men on the highway. That would be your style, but they are big boys and can take care of themselves. Go spend some time with your family. It's Dr. Dalry, right? Department head at Saint Antoine Hospital, right?"

The news had spread throughout the building. Nico's superior officer stood up with a smile.

"I wish you much happiness, Chief."

"Thank you, Commissioner."

"I won't be here much longer either. Mr. Monthalet is waiting for me, and it's Friday night," she said with a hint of softness in her voice.

Once she was gone, Nico followed suit, gathering his things and exchanging his dress shoes for boots.

Outside, Nico looked at his watch. Caroline would be finishing her shift soon. Why not take her out to dinner? He imagined himself talking with her, listening to her laugh, watching her lips move, drowning in her eyes. He wanted her, a feeling that was magnified by the simple fact that he couldn't have her there and then.

18

"Sirs, we are finished here," Armelle Vilars said.

Kriven breathed a sigh of relief. Nico could see that the night spent exhuming the body and then following the hearse more than a hundred miles to Paris had exhausted the man. Attending the subsequent autopsy had clearly done him in.

Nico looked away from the body, which was no more than a pile of bones and bits of burned tissue, and put a hand on Kriven's shoulder. "That's enough, David. Go home and get some rest."

The detective did not resist. He turned and left. Autopsies were always acts of violence.

"My report will be on your desk first thing Monday morning, Magistrate Becker," Vilars said, removing her latex gloves.

"It looks like you won't be getting any break during the month of December," Alexandre Becker said.

"Tell me about it," Vilars said. "I can confirm that business here in the morgue is as brisk as ever. And La Crim' is finding even more for me to do, with this murder accusation hidden in a molar."

Nico winked at his friend.

"I'll go change," she said.

Nico was also eager to get to the locker room. The smell of death and disinfectant was clinging to his skin. He needed a good shower with half a bottle of soap.

"A finely executed autopsy, as usual," Alexandre said.

"Yes," Nico responded.

Christophe Parize had died in a car accident, and his scorched body had not been recognizable. The fire had consumed his arms first, making it impossible to check the fingerprints. The blaze had been so hot, even his teeth were destroyed. Dental records, therefore, couldn't be used to identify him. The fire had also emptied the eye sockets and burned the victim's hair. Intestines were tougher, Armelle said with a touch of dark humor. They could burst. There were some less-damaged areas, primarily the genitals, because the victim was sitting at the time of the accident. It was clear, though, that the victim was Caucasian. The license plate on the car, along with Christopher Parize's personal effects, notably his floral boxer shorts, had been used to identify him.

Decomposition had played its role. The body had mummified, leaking water, fat, and blood. Bacteria had proliferated, and necrophagous insects had made their way into the coffin, eating the organs and soft tissue. In the end, only some of the burned bones remained in decent shape. Strangely, however, the smell was bearable. As Armelle said, put a dead fish on the balcony, and it would stink for the first three months. After that, it wouldn't smell so bad.

Armelle had set out the skeleton on the autopsy table and numbered the bones. The lack of artificial implants, prostheses, and damage caused by illness or injury had hindered identification. She had been able to determine approximate age, sex, and ethnicity, all of which corresponded with those of Dr. Parize, but nothing could definitively determine the identity. DNA analysis was the only way, and the professor had removed a piece of the femur, a deep bone wrapped in thick muscle. DNA was a sturdy molecule, so resistant that archeologists had dated some from more than a 130 million years earlier. Unwound, the double helix would be about six feet long. Folded, it could fit into the minuscule nucleus of a cell.

For a long time, Nico had relied on Nantes University for this kind of analysis. Fifteen or so years earlier, the lab there had mastered the technique and had been recognized the world over for its reliable results. The police forensics lab in Paris had lacked the means to do such thorough analysis. But things had changed. The university lab was working less and less with police organizations, while the National Police Forensics Institute was investing heavily in research and development. The facilities had been modernized, and evidence processing had been streamlined. Charles Queneau had hired Dr. Tom Robin, one of Europe's best molecular biologists. Robin would work over the weekend to get the DNA results to Nico.

The autopsy had been highly methodical. It had, however, taken an unexpected turn when Vilars had found a .22-caliber long-rifle bullet in the victim's skull.

Kriven had then called it: a barbecue. That was when a murder victim was tossed into a car, and the car was set ablaze to thwart identification and destroy evidence. It was simple and effective. No X-rays had been taken at the time, and with the extent of the burns, nobody had noticed the bullet in the man's head. But Vilars was a pro. She left nothing uncovered.

Becker and Nico exited the building and inhaled the crisp winter air. Nico started when he heard the voice of Captain Vidal.

"I'm here, Chief."

Vidal had come to pick up the bullet and take it to forensics, which would check it for the same markings found on the bullet from Guedj's skull. That would help to determine if it had been fired by the Unique DES 69 retrieved from the pharmacist's home.

"Did you do what I asked?" Nico asked.

"Yes, I got samples from the home of Christophe Parize's ex-wife. She had kept some of his things. If that is not enough, we could still get saliva from the children. I'll give Robin the samples. He'll be able to compare."

"Then at least we'll know," Magistrate Becker said.

"I'll get the stuff and go," Vidal said. He'd have to hurry if they expected to have the results by the following day.

The police chief and the investigating magistrate walked to their cars, which were parked next to each other.

"What do you think?" Becker asked.

"The poor fellow in the car was shot, and his murder was made to look like an accident. After that, he was buried in the Parize family vault. Then, by pure coincidence, Guedj ran into his old friend in a bookstore. Do you know what Albert Einstein said about coincidence? It's God's way of remaining anonymous. I like that. If you ask me, I wouldn't bet a kopeck that the good Dr. Parize is dead."

"Parize or not, we have another murder on our hands. And at least we have something to go on. Let's step on it."

"I suggest a visit to Parize's ex-wife. She might know what he was doing at the bookstore on September 15."

"If he's not the one in the morgue, of course. Anything else?"

"Saint Louis Hospital. We need to question the staff in the hematology-oncology department. And we'll have to bring in those close to Parize for questioning."

"I'll get your orders signed and on your desk within the hour."

The magistrate was giving up his Saturday and expected Nico to do the same.

"Perfect. I'll get everything going." A ringtone interrupted. Nicole Monthalet's number appeared on the screen. "Sirsky here."

"I've got the paper in front of me," she said. "Let me read the headline. 'A dead man's tooth lives to tell the tale.' The article is juicy: 'It all began with a terse message hidden under a bad filling, discovered at the Paris Medical School on the Rue des Saints-Pères, known for its ghoulish student pranks. What happened to the dead pharmacist who gave his body to science? Should the message "I was murdered" be taken seriously? The Paris Criminal Investigation Division will have to decide. Was this the only way the victim, knowing he was in danger, could trap his predators?'"

Nicole Monthalet was silent for a moment. "You can read the rest yourself. The Guedj family will find out soon, as will the killers."

"I'll call Mrs. Guedj immediately."

"Reporters will be harassing headquarters. They'll want to talk to you. They know you're heading the investigation. I'll do what I can to buy us some time. But they'll get to you. The interior minister will be doing you-know-what in his pants, if you get my meaning, and when that happens, it's never a good sign for the prefect or for us."

"I'm aware of that, Commissioner."

"We could suggest that it was a bad joke played by a seriously depressed man. I don't see how else we can keep the vultures away and make the culprits think we're not pursuing the case. We'll have to convince his wife and kids that this is the best strategy. And we can't count on sticking with this story indefinitely, or we'll risk losing our credibility. Fix this quick, Chief."

She ended the call. What else could she say? Reporters and politics were part and parcel of the job.

"Is there a problem?" Becker asked.

"We've made the front page again. Our molar mystery."

"Oops. The prosecutor must be getting ready to call me."

"What about the independence of the justice system?"

"I'm trying. I'm trying," Becker said as he slid behind the wheel of his car. "Call me when you've got something."

"Will do. I know how much you love to hear the sound of my voice."

Nico got into his own car, and they both headed off toward the Île de la Cité.

Later in the afternoon, Nico rang the bell at Mrs. Parize's home in the fifteenth arrondissement, a well-rested Franck Plassard by his side.

Christophe Parize's ex-wife opened the door and scowled when they showed their badges. "He keeps on giving me grief, even from the grave."

They followed her into the kitchen, where she offered them chairs. No living room for them, certainly a sign that the woman had bitter memories of her children's father.

"Was it a tough divorce?" Plassard asked.

She shot him a look. "Tough? You've got to be kidding. He ruined my life. A real bastard."

Nico tried to steer the conversation in another direction. "How old are your children?"

"They're nineteen. Twins." Her face had brightened a bit at the mention of her children, and Nico thought they might get somewhere if they talked about the kids.

"Marine is a brilliant student. She's getting ready to enter an elite business school. Olivier is studying law."

"You must be proud of them."

"Very. It's a good thing I have them. I haven't told them anything—about the exhumation, I mean. But this morning, some police captain showed up to get DNA from some things of his that I still have. Do I get an explanation? What's this all about?"

She was playing with a box of matches. The room was decorated with wreaths, garland, candles, and an Advent calendar, all in Christmas colors. A basket of wrapped packages was on the floor, next to the table. But this conversation felt better suited for Halloween.

"We have some questions concerning your ex-husband's death."

"What do you mean? Like hit and run? Someone killed him?"

If only she knew, Nico thought.

"Something like that."

"You're being a little mysterious, Inspector. I have a right to know."

The woman was a paralegal, and her professional reflexes were kicking in. It was best to be frank.

"The man found in your ex-husband's car did not die in the accident and the subsequent fire."

"What did he die of?"

"He was shot."

Silence fell.

"Why do you say 'the man'? You're not sure that it was Christophe?"

"The DNA tests will confirm whether it was or wasn't your ex-husband," Plassard said.

"You need confirmation—now, all this time after his funeral?" She stood up, reached for a glass from a cupboard, and filled it with water from the tap.

"It's so... so outrageous. Do you think he ran across the wrong person on the road?"

"It could be any number of things," Nico said.

"What exactly do you want to know?"

"Do you remember anything special happening on September 15?"

She stared at Nico. "What day?" she managed to get out. She was shaking, and Nico read fear on her face. What was she afraid of?

Nico asked as gently as he could. "What happened on that day, ma'am?"

"My daughter, Marine…. There was a reception for her at the Lycée Louis-le-Grand on the Rue Saint-Jacques to honor her for getting first place in the national math examination."

The Rue Saint-Jacques was just a few minutes from the Vigot-Maloine bookstore.

"That's a great honor," Nico said, feigning enthusiasm in the hope that she would continue talking. "What kind of relationship did your ex-husband have with your children?"

"His death hit both Marine and Olivier hard, of course. But they blamed him for what happened between us."

"Is he the one who decided to leave?"

She sighed. "I kicked him out. He was insufferable, and we hadn't really been a couple for a long time."

"Who was he closer to? Your daughter?"

"You're scaring me. Yes, probably Marine. Olivier couldn't put up with his father's silent and disagreeable attitude and his lack of respect for me. They fought a lot."

Plassard interrupted. "Didn't it bother Marine too?"

"Of course it did!" Mrs. Parize protested. "It affected her even more, because she admired her father, Dr. Parize, the celebrated hematologist. She was always trying to impress him, to get his attention with her good grades."

"Did it work?"

"He bragged about his daughter all the time, except his last few months, when he was totally focused on his job and the hospital. The attention he gave Marine must have hurt Olivier, but he never said anything. He loves his sister too much to complain."

"Would Christophe have wanted to be there on September 15?" Nico asked.

"My God! What are you suggesting? That he's alive? That he might have tried to see Marine on that day? That he's lurking? You're really scaring me now."

"Calm down, ma'am," Plassard said.

"*Calm down!* How would you react in my shoes?"

"The same, I'm sure," Nico said. "That is why we want to clarify the situation."

"I don't have anything else to say. I thought Christophe was dead and buried, and now you come along and re-suscitate him."

"Nobody is being resuscitated, Mrs. Parize."

"Yet someone must have seen him near the school on the day of the reception, or why would you be asking all these questions?"

Nico and Plassard stood up.

"Are we done here? Are you leaving?"

"We will keep you informed," Nico said. "In the meantime, please don't worry."

"That's easy for you to say."

"I'm aware of that, ma'am. One thing is for sure. If your ex-husband is alive, he wouldn't want to hurt Marine, or Olivier, or you."

"You're right," she conceded, accompanying Nico and Plassard to the door.

Nico was truly troubled. If Christophe Parize had not died in Burgundy, if some other man had been murdered and placed in his car, then this was premeditated first-degree murder. Could Dr. Parize have come up with this scheme? Did he have it in him? And why? To disappear and start his life over somewhere else? If so, why was he still keeping track of his daughter? Why would he risk being found out by trying to catch a glimpse of her on a very important day? And would he have been capable of orchestrating Guedj's suicide? Who was the man who went to the pharmacy to intimidate Guedj? Did he have an accomplice in the job? But what job?

What damned job?

19

Things were falling apart. If only he had been more clearheaded, more farsighted, he would have guessed that this would happen. But he had so wanted to conquer his adversary, to win the wild gamble he had made. He was used to success. It was only natural to assume that he would succeed this time. Now he was on the edge of a cliff. But what did it matter in the end? He was no longer afraid of emptiness. He wanted to die when the time came. Soon. Very soon. Wasn't it just a question of days now? He clenched his fists in anger, and the blood rushed to his cheeks. The rage of the vanquished.

He had not been up to the challenge this time. And yet, it was one of the most important battles he would have to fight. The others—the struggles that had helped him build an empire, to become filthy rich, to dominate the world—were nothing in comparison with the fight he was about to lose. His life was going up in smoke, and all his work would be in vain. His bitter laughter bounced off the walls. And tears rose to his eyes.

He turned to his employee, his chief security officer. The man was loyal, ready to do anything to pay back the debt he thought he owed. Hadn't he given this man a chance when everyone else had dropped him? He had always taken full advantage of his leverage, and they both knew it.

"Who ordered the exhumation?" he asked. He needed to put a name on his torturer.

"Magistrate Alexandre Becker. Chief Nico Sirsky of the Criminal Investigation Division is running the investigation."

"Chief Sirsky. His name was in the paper. 'Dead man's tooth lives to tell the tale.' That was the headline. Guedj would have liked it. That sneaky pharmacist really got me. Hat's off to him."

"If Parize hadn't taken so many liberties, we wouldn't be where we are now."

"Don't be so stupid. Sooner or later, word would have gotten out. I was so smug."

"No, sir," the man dressed in black said. "It was just despair."

He sighed. "I wanted to defy God himself."

"You were not the only one responsible."

His eyes widened. His employee was right. All the blood on his hands—wasn't that the cost of what he had needed to do? It was time to settle up. Did he have a choice?

"What are your orders, sir?"

"We need to take care of it. There's no going back." His voice was barely a whisper.

"Yes, sir."

"Sirsky's going to make things tough."

"That's for sure."

"He's the kind of guy who doesn't let go. He likes to impress people."

"Yes, I believe so. But we're not there yet, and maybe we won't ever be."

"With a little luck. But I ran out of luck a long time ago."

"Not necessarily, sir."

"Go. Keep me posted."

The man in black disappeared. Someone with a vaguely familiar face entered the room. The face was gaunt, closed, older. It was astonishing how pain built walls between people, high impassable walls topped with watchtowers.

20

On Monday, twelve days after the message hidden in Bruno Guedj's tooth had been found, some force led him to the Rue des Saint-Pères. He probably needed to go back to the beginning.

Nico knew the area well, so well, he was feeling like a dinosaur, like Debauve and Gallais, which had been making "*chocolats fins et hygiéniques*" since the turn of the nineteenth century at 30 Rue des Saint-Pères. It was a bustling neighborhood that had been built around the Abbey of Saint-Germain-des-Prés and influenced by the Deux-Magots, Café de Flore, and Brasserie Lipp, the haunts of intellectuals and artists after the Second World War. Nico had spent a lot of time in these places. He had often walked past the Paris Descartes University Medical School. The students he saw crowded around 45 Rue des Saint-Pères on this day didn't seem much different from the students he had gone to school with.

Nico approached the monumental bronze doors known as the Porte de la Science. They were nearly twenty-six feet tall and half as wide. Bas-reliefs depicted the appearance of life, animals both fighting and mating, and Adam and Eve chased from paradise. Asclepius, the god of medicine, dominated the tympan above the doors. At his feet, people begged the god for healing.

Nico entered the building and made his way into the crowded hallway, filled not only with students, but also with display panels and a huge Christmas tree. Young people were studying on benches and around tables under the staircases. A stranger in this place, Nico climbed the stairs without raising any curiosity. Security would be a near impossibility here, he thought, and paradoxically, this reassured him. As much of a cop as he was, he hated the idea of living in a society where everyone was under constant surveillance. He looked through an open door to an enormous room. On the board, he saw "Cournot-Nash Equilibrium" and scrawling that looked like gibberish to him. Farther down the hall, a herd was forming at the Claude Bernard lecture hall.

He finally reached the sixth floor and walked past the body donation office. At the end of the hallway, the large red off-limits door pulled him like a magnet. Marcel's lair. He went past the Farabeuf and Poirier labs and then beyond the "staff only" Stairwell H. He knocked. The tech, looking focused and grumpy, opened the door.

"Ah, what brings you, Inspector?"

To tell the truth, Nico didn't really know.

Marcel tried again. "Did you see Mrs. Bordieu?"

"No, I didn't want to bother her."

"Oh," Marcel said, frowning. Then he smiled. "Do you want to come in?"

"May I?"

"In theory, no, not without my boss's okay, but you aren't just anybody. So I think I can let you in. We don't have to go and tell everyone about it, right?" Marcel winked.

"Fine by me," Nico said, stepping into what seemed like another dimension.

The first thing that struck Nico were the man's hands—thick, powerful hands—and his immaculate white coat.

"I like everything spick-and-span," Marcel said, inviting Nico into his lab, which was a small, fully equipped kitchen.

"How did you end up here?"

"You looking for a job? The university is going to have to replace me soon."

Nico grinned. The man was a joker.

"I started out as a butcher at the Villette slaughterhouses. Yep, believe it or not. At least I got some real training. And then, one day, well, opportunity makes the thief. So much was possible at the time. Today, they'd never hire a butcher."

This was almost unbelievable. A butcher right here, in the medical school. The last beef to come out of the Villette slaughterhouses was butchered in 1974. Marcel had left the huge Grande Halle and its 333 acres of constantly bustling and noisy grounds for this silent space containing three walk-in cold rooms filled with human remains. His knowledge of dismemberment and his love for a job well done had arrived with him.

"I've got to take a leg to the seventh floor. Would you like to come with me?"

"I'm right behind you."

Marcel walked into one of the cold rooms. Nico stood at the door and peered at what was inside. He began to hyperventilate and feel lightheaded. The butcher turned around.

"You've seen worse, haven't you?"

"I'm not sure about that," Nico said. His legs were weak.

Marcel raised his voice. "Step back."

The order hit Nico like a slap in the face. He moved back down the hallway and leaned his forehead against a cool window. But the vision of horror was stuck in his brain: massive gray metal shelves, nude bodies piled up, decapitated heads, an old lady, all skin and bone, in a fetal position. The only thing missing were the butcher's hooks.

This was where Bruno Guedj chose to go after his death. He even knew what awaited him, unlike most of the people who donated their bodies to science. Some tech had cut off his head and set it on one of the racks in this dark, frigid place. Fortunately, Marcel was a nice fellow who liked things spick-and-span and respected the dead. Nico shuddered at the thought of what a cold room managed by someone who was less meticulous would look like. He knew he wouldn't want anyone but Marcel to take care of him if, by chance, he ended up in this school feet first.

Nico started at the sound of a cart. It was covered with a blue sheet.

"You feeling better, chap? Me, I wouldn't want to see some dude that's just been bumped off. A woman or child would be worse. Don't know how you do it. I'm so used to this, I can't imagine how it could shock anyone."

"Sorry."

"Don't worry. I should have warned you."

"You've got quite a job there."

"I wouldn't change it for anything. Watching over them puts my mind at ease. Who will do it when I'm gone?" Marcel walked through the red door and headed toward the dumbwaiter.

Nico changed the subject. "What do you think about the message in the tooth?"

"I heard what they're saying on TV. Do you believe that theory?"

"Apparently you don't."

"We're on the same wavelength, my friend. The man with the filling was throwing a bottle out to sea. We did our jobs and caught the bottle. Now Subject 510 is 10-35."

Nico laughed at his reference to the major-crime-alert scanner code. It would have made a great headline in a paper, but for that, the copy desk would have needed to know about Marcel.

Once out of the elevator, Marcel typed in a door code. "Here, we have small work labs and a larger central room for embalming. We'll have to go through it."

"No problem."

Inside, a series of sinks filled an entire wall. Four bodies lay on tables, tubes connecting them to strange machines. They were skin and bones, ugly and terrifying.

"Those pumps inject a chemical solution into the arteries. We use formol, which is a ten percent solution of formaldehyde. We inject through the carotid. The process stops bacteria and keeps the cells from breaking down. The procedure also pushes out the blood and other body fluids that cause decomposition. The fluids drain out through the jugular vein."

Two masked men walked over.

"Is the subject ready?" one of them asked.

Marcel tapped on the blue sheet and led them into a small room, where he took the limb and placed it on an operating table. One of the surgeons adjusted the operating lamp to light up the knee, while the other picked up a scalpel. Marcel closed the door on his way out.

Nico took a deep breath once they were out of the embalming room. This butcher-turned-body-processor lived in another world altogether.

"Someone killed 510, didn't they?" Marcel said. "He seemed like an ordinary guy. What do you think happened to him?"

"He met up with an old college friend."

"That's all? Is that enough to get bumped off?"

"Except that college friend died in a car accident more than a year ago. Everybody thought he was dead and buried."

"Did he kick the bucket or didn't he?"

"We exhumed the body and autopsied it. The old friend in question never died on the road."

There was no disputing DNA tests. The man found burned in Dr. Christophe Parize's vehicle was not Christophe Parize. So who was he? The lab was running the results through the national DNA database, created in 1998 and shared by the police and the gendarmerie. It was designed to help find culprits and missing persons. Parize's replacement, however, was still unknown.

Marcel whistled. "You don't do anything halfway, do you? That's quite a job you've got there."

"I wouldn't change it for anything. It puts my mind at ease to catch the bad guys."

The return to the outside world felt like a shock to Nico's system. It was a strange sensation, and he wondered how Marcel made the transition every day. He had to come back to reality, to the unidentified body found in Christophe Parize's car. And most of all, to this basic question: why had the doctor's disappearance been staged? If he answered that, he most likely could solve Bruno Guedj's murder. The pharmacist wasn't supposed to know that his friend was alive, and certainly, he wasn't supposed to start turning things upside down to find him. Bruno Guedj's death notice had been signed in the coincidence that caused him to cross paths with his old school buddy.

Practically speaking, nothing linked the fake suicide to the burned body in the car. The .22-caliber long-rifle bullets taken from the respective skulls hadn't matched up, so the Unique DES 69 hadn't been used on the John Doe. Too bad. That said, whoever came up with the diabolical plan to erase Dr. Christophe Parize from the face of the earth had a major problem. That problem was La Crim'. Now that Nico and his team had picked up the scent, they wouldn't let go.

As Nico put some distance between the Paris Descartes University and himself, between the cold rooms at the school and the winter vista outside, his mind returned to Sylvie. Jacqueline and André had talked to their daughter. She had cried at the sound of their voices. Sylvie was feeling better, and she missed Dimitri. But she had to do more than miss her son. She had to be his mother, drug-free and emotionally healthy—present in every sense of the word. No one could take her place. The pharmacist's sons had lost one of their parents. They would always suffer for it. Nico intended to do whatever he could to ensure that Dimitri had two parents who were fully engaged in his life.

Nico parked in front of police headquarters. On the other side of the Seine, a travel agency on the Quai des Grands Augustins was teasing him again. What was he waiting for? All he had to do was cross the river, go into the agency, and buy the tickets. Wait, and it could be too late, as it almost had been three months ago. Too late could happen at any time. "But where should we go?" he wondered. To a spot where he could watch Caroline run along the beach and wade in a blue ocean? Or an enchanted place he could introduce her and Dimitri to—a place that would make Anya's eyes glisten and make his sister Tanya's heart beat faster? For now, though, he needed to let the fantasy go.

He walked through the door on the Quai des Orfèvres. Deputy Chief Jean-Marie Rost met him as he was going into his office.

"Can I talk to you for a minute?"

"Of course. Come in."

"Did you just come back from the med school?"

"That's right."

"And?"

"Nothing special."

"Are you pulling my leg? You don't do anything without something in mind."

"I just needed to think about the case. I talked to Marcel."

"The guy who prepares the bodies? Vidal and Almeida told me about him. I think that weirdo left a lifetime impression on them."

"I get that, believe me. Do you have any news from Christophe Parize's parents?"

"That's why I wanted to see you. They'll be in this afternoon."

"Who's handling them?"

"Kriven, unless you want someone else on it."

"No. David is perfect. Do you have an update from him?"

Nico had sent Kriven and his team to Saint Louis Hospital, where Parize had worked. Saint Louis Hospital had been built at the beginning of the seventeenth century to quarantine those struck by the plague. Over the centuries, the hospital's mission and medical offerings had expanded considerably. It now provided a full range of care and boasted nearly 600 beds. Dr. Parize had been one of the hospital's more than 3,200 employees. Among them were 780 doctors, including five specialists in the hematology-oncology department. Nico felt sure that at least one or two of them had something to say about their former colleague, who had so abruptly disappeared.

"They're still at the hospital, digging for information," Rost said.

"I hope they reel in a big fish."

"They'd better. Clearly, the divorce was not enough to explain his disappearance or the car accident and burned body."

"That's what I'm thinking. Not with Parize being so attached to his daughter. He must have had a really good reason. Did you reach the lycée?"

"Yes, I went to Louis-le-Grand. Marine is in a preparatory class. I also made an appointment with the head of the math prizewinners association she belongs to. Nobody noticed anybody stalking the girl, and nobody has seen Dr. Parize since his presumed death. However, Marine continues to include her dad's profession in all the paperwork she has to fill out, as if nothing ever happened to him."

"The father's admiration for his daughter gives us something to go on. He was proud of her, so much so that he took the risk of trying to catch a glimpse of her at the reception in her honor. We have to question her. We don't have a choice, and I have this strange feeling—"

"I agree."

Rost's cell phone rang, interrupting the conversation. He put it on speakerphone.

"Chief?" a woman's voice said.

"Yes, what's going on?" It was Commander Charlotte Maurin, the new recruit who had replaced Hureau.

"Some funny business near the Île aux Cygnes."

"What is it?"

"A man weighed down with an anchor, near the pier."

"That's no fun."

"He's dead."

"An important detail."

"He looks like the twin brother of the guy whose photo you gave us. His features are a little puffy, but the resemblance is there."

Neither Nico nor Rost responded.

"Chief?"

"We're on our way," Rost said, ending the call.

21

Just going into a place like this made his hands clammy. David Kriven worked in a world full of horrors. He was constantly exposed to violence, tears, and blood. But this was unbearable, and the energy he needed to cover up his discomfort was taking almost everything he had.

On the Avenue Claude Vellefaux, the Saint Louis Hospital security guards opened the gate and let Kriven and Vidal park in the inside lot, which was off limits to visitors. Behind them, in another car, were Lieutenant Almeida and Plassard.

The few yards between his car and the main hospital building were enough to spike Kriven's blood pressure. The spacious modern lobby, with its high glass-topped ceiling that let the daylight in was not enough to calm him. It had the opposite effect, as did the cafeteria and the exhibit recounting the hospital's storied history. The sight of women wearing turbans to cover their bald skulls, patients clinging to their rolling IV carts, gaunt figures, and empty eyes panicked him. So did the signs to the different wings of the hospital. They all pointed to death row, as far as he was concerned. In the midst of this jumble, people in white coats circulated with swift, determined steps. Nothing dared to impede their drive to heal. In general, Kriven kept his distance from people of that species. They brought bad luck.

Kriven led his team to the elevator. The hematology-oncology wing was on the seventh floor. Just as the doors began to close, Kriven caught a nauseating whiff of coffee. He spotted a young man in a bathrobe and slippers stooped in front of the coffee machine. He was so pale, it was scary. The elevator shook as it started taking them up. Kriven had the feeling he was trapped in a crypt.

"You're not looking so good," Almeida said.

"He doesn't like elevators," Vidal said.

"The smell of antiseptic doesn't help," Plassard said.

The ride up seemed overly long. Lieutenant Almeida cleared his throat several times in the silence.

"I don't smell anything," Vidal said.

The elevator finally arrived on the right floor. Kriven was saved, for the moment, at least. They entered the wing where Dr. Parize had practiced medicine before giving it up for no apparent reason, before staging his accident and passing himself off as dead, before some poor fellow named Bruno Guedj had gotten himself killed simply because they had met by chance in a bookstore.

"Can I help you?" a nurse asked, looking surprised to see the four detectives.

Kriven showed his badge. "We called ahead."

"Oh, you're the detectives. We freed up an office for you. Shall I take you there?"

"We would like to question the doctors one by one."

"I'll let our department head know right away. I don't know how it's been organized."

Kriven ordered the team to go through the halls and discreetly question the staff. He would handle the five specialists. In circles where professional and patient privacy reigned, getting information required a certain amount of cleverness. If there was information to get. Kriven bet there was.

The first man to sit down with him was barely over thirty, his own age. Kriven wondered if he would trust the young man with his life. Kriven knew it wasn't the same in his line of work. His people were already dead. All he had to do was catch the guys who murdered them.

"You worked with Dr. Parize. I would like to ask you a few questions about him," Kriven began.

"I was transferred here a year before he disappeared, so I didn't know him well," the doctor said, point blank.

Kriven figured the doctor was hoping he would let him go without asking many questions. But this man was the perfect kind of person to interview, because he didn't seem to have any emotional bonds with his former colleague. Kriven thought he might even be willing to share some stories.

"A year was enough time for someone like you to form an opinion of the man."

The doctor started blinking. Kriven knew he was making the young physician nervous.

"First, give me your general opinion of Dr. Parize. What kind of doctor was he?"

"A very good one. Really. I learned a lot from him."

"I imagine that you have to be very ambitious to end up here. Ambitious and talented."

"That's correct. Saint Louis Hospital is known the world over for its work in the area of hematology. Professors Jean Bernard and Jean Dausset were our fore-runners, and we are continuing their work."

"So was Dr. Parize a worthy successor, in your opinion?"

"I…I would say so."

He had hesitated. Kriven pushed. "That's strange. You seem to have some doubts."

"It's just that he changed after we met."

"How is that?"

"He became curt and irritable."

"With you?"

"With the entire team."

"Did he have family problems?"

"Uh, there were rumors, but I couldn't tell you if they were true or not."

"Rumors, you say. What kind of rumors?"

"That he was getting a divorce."

"Your source was reliable. And did he have any problems professionally?"

The young man looked down for an instant. He fiddled with a pen. "Things weren't going the way he wanted them to," he finally said.

"I'm sure that you can be more precise."

"The boss was on the verge of leaving, and Dr. Parize wanted his job."

"Which job?"

"Department head."

"So he applied for the position and didn't get it?"

"That's right," the doctor responded.

"Who made the decision?"

"The board."

"What reason did they give?"

"His family situation."

"Oops. You mean they didn't want to give divorced physicians that kind of responsibility?"

"I said he had changed. I suppose his behavior wasn't appropriate."

"Who was the lucky person to get the job?"

"Dr. Christine Sahian. She's very competent."

"Okay, please send in one of your colleagues."

"It's a real confessional here. What about Dr. Sahian?"

"We'll save the best for last."

Franck Plassard had chosen to interview a gray-haired nurse, one old enough to know the ins and outs of the hospital and some truths that were better left unsaid. He used his charm to draw out the woman, who looked about the same age as his mother. Pierre Vidal walked by and gave him a wink.

"I liked Christophe. I knew him when he was just a kid. He didn't deserve to die in a car accident. I'm still upset over it. I guess nobody deserves that, right?"

"You're right, nobody."

"The law of series. It's so sad."

A red flag. Plassard paused. "The law of series?"

"You know. When a random event happens more than once in a short period of time, and there doesn't seem to be any logical explanation."

"I'm not following, ma'am."

"Doctors killed in accidents, dying unfairly when they've dedicated their lives to healing others."

As if dedicating your life to helping others shielded anyone from danger.

"Who are you talking about, ma'am?"

The Île aux Cygnes was nothing more than a strip of artificial land. It was built in the nineteenth century and was now a promenade about a half mile long and less than forty feet wide, lined with trees and peppered with benches. It was best known for harboring a small replica of the Statue of Liberty, which the United States gave to France on the hundredth anniversary of the French Revolution.

Nico and Jean-Marie Rost rushed down the steps of the Viaduc de Passy, crossed the police line, and headed toward the rusty landing stage. The island, which offered a view of Trocadéro and its fountains, had a pier for barges that gave dinner cruises. At the moment, a patrol boat belonging to the river brigade occupied the pier. Divers were already searching the waters for evidence. Commander Charlotte Maurin's squad was busy around the body that had been pulled from the water.

"Who discovered the body?" Rost asked.

"The river patrol. We couldn't have been luckier," Maurin said.

This unit was based on the Quai Saint-Bernard and answered to police operational and technical services. Its officers had training in water-related areas, such as piloting, diving, and boat mechanics. The chief of the unit was a former diver and explosives expert with the national marine. Their mission was to ensure the safety of people and goods on the waterways in the capital and the area surrounding Paris. They were nicknamed the Saint Bernards.

"They discovered it during a routine inspection."

"What state was it in?" Nico asked.

"Identifiable. Clearly drowned."

Immersion changed the normal process of decomposition. It slowed significantly in cold water and accelerated once the body was removed, as if the body were trying to catch up. In winter, the Seine ranged from thirty-five to forty degrees and acted like a refrigerator.

"The river patrol pulled the body up to the bank before we arrived and noted epistaxis. That's a nosebleed and an indication that the victim could have been beaten before death."

They walked over to the corpse, which was in a body bag that would protect it from outside elements that might alter the evidence. The man's face was purple, and fluid was dribbling from his mouth. One of his ears was torn, probably eaten by a rodent. His hands were wrapped in plastic bags to keep the wrinkled skin from slipping like gloves off his bones. Maurin held out a picture of Christophe Parize, which police around the country had received the day before. They looked from the picture to the victim several times.

"It's him," Rost said. "Did you find anything in the surrounding area?"

"Nothing important. Some cigarette butts and a gum wrapper that could belong to anyone."

"And the anchor keeping him under?" Nico asked.

"The divers picked it up. We'll get it to the lab."

"Brr. It's freezing," Rost grumbled. "No time to be taking a dip."

"The officer who processed the crime noted footprints in the snow, but who do they belong to? The murderers? The river patrol? People out walking? Frankly, I just told him to forget it," Maurin said. "It's a lot of work for no reason, since we've got nothing to compare them to."

Rost nodded.

Maurin continued. "We'll go over the island with a fine-tooth comb. Backup from the river patrol should be here any minute. But I don't have much hope."

Nico agreed. They now knew they were dealing with an organized group. And the weather was not helping them.

"They can go," Nico said, looking at the officers responsible for taking the body.

Maurin gave the officers the signal, and they zipped up the bag. The corpse disappeared.

"Has someone informed Professor Vilars?"

"She's getting ready to do the autopsy," Maurin answered.

With accelerated decomposition, she had to act quickly.

"Good work, Charlotte. Keep us posted," Nico said.

The two men walked back toward the Bir-Hakeim Bridge.

"Christophe Parize! It's completely crazy," Rost said.

"That proves one thing: we're headed in the right direction. The murderers may have been able to get rid of Bruno Guedj, but they can't get in the way of our investigation."

"Do you think they were trying to buy some time?"

"They opted for a temporary solution: eliminating the weak link, or Parize. They're afraid. And they must have a lot to lose to take that kind of risk."

§ § §

The atmosphere had changed at headquarters. The molar mystery had become a high-profile case. Although the detectives felt as though they had entered a dense, dark forest full of ghosts—a forest that at least two other people had gotten lost in—they were confident that they would find the signposts pointing the way to the culprits.

Magistrate Becker joined Nico in his office. "Now we have proof that someone else—and probably more people, as well—were involved in the disappearance of Christophe Parize. He didn't instigate his vanishing act all by himself."

"I never really thought he had the profile of someone who would find a replacement for himself and stage a car accident," Nico said. "The good doctor must have been a pawn in a much larger operation. On September 15, while he was in Paris, Bruno Guedj recognized him, indirectly exposing his accomplices."

"Who then decided to get rid of the pharmacist."

"But we discovered Guedj's message, and they started losing their grip."

"We sentenced Christophe Parize to his death when we got involved," Becker sighed.

"We're facing some very determined people."

"We'll still need to make sure it's Parize who was fished out of the Seine."

"Believe me, the drowned man looked exactly like him. Kriven's back. Should I call him in?"

"Yes, let's review the case."

Looking grim, David Kriven sank into a chair. "I hate hospitals. They stink. I feel like I'm covered with the smell. And all those sick people—"

Everyone knew Kriven was a hypochondriac. He would be the object of much teasing over his trip to the hospital, and that would help to release some of the tension of the investigation.

Kriven began. "Dr. Parize was a specialist in hematology and oncology. To give you some background, we all know what oncology is. Hematology involves not only the study of blood, but also the study of bone marrow and the lymph system. Both areas of specialization are often involved in the treatment of diseases such as lymphoma and leukemia. The hospital has made a name for itself in hematology and oncology, and it takes pride in its research. According to the people we questioned, the doctor was a well-liked, competent professional who was dedicated to the hospital. He was a valued member of the team."

"So Dr. Parize was perfect?" Becker asked.

"Not entirely. A few months before his death, the doc became a regular Mr. Hyde."

"And you know why, of course," Nico said. He was getting impatient.

"He got passed up for department head. It made him very angry, nearly paranoid, convinced that his colleagues were conspiring against him. Then they named a woman to the position, which didn't help."

"His wife was giving him trouble at home, and here comes another woman getting in his way," Becker said.

"Exactly. When his new superior recommended that he take a few days off to cool down, Parize lost it. The argument was heard all over the wing. Strangely, after he stomped off, he came back and said he would take the leave."

"Let me guess. That's when he died," Nico said.

"And the chief wins the stove and refrigerator behind the curtain," Kriven said.

"Is there anything else?" Becker asked.

"In fact, Magistrate Becker, there may be something else," Kriven said with a smile. "Maybe something. I'm not sure. Three weeks before the accident, a bigwig from the hospital, Professor Claude Janin, disappeared."

"How did he disappear?" Becker asked.

"His yacht caught on fire in the Mediterranean. The bodies were never found."

Nico reacted. "Bodies?"

"The dude was having a grand old time with his mistress, a nurse he'd been seeing for ten or so years. Her name was Danièle Lemaire. Everyone in the hospital knew about the affair."

It was Becker's turn to react. "Ten years! Now that's a double life."

"Yep. He had been married for thirty-six years, had three kids, a dog, and two goldfish."

"And the nurse?" Nico asked.

"She worked at Saint Louis, too. Unmarried, no kids, no dog, no goldfish. No ties. She was desperately hoping the big kahuna would leave his family and his comfortable life for her. Now they are finally united."

"That's three deaths in three weeks at the same hospital," Becker said. "Quite a hit for one hospital to take. What do you know about this bigwig?"

"His résumé is as long as my arm. Very impressive. He ran one of the hospital labs, along with a research unit, and he taught immunology at Paris Diderot University. He spent a number of years in the United States, where he made major discoveries in histocompatibility. Sorry, don't ask me what that means. I didn't have time to look it up. These dudes blow me away. He was fifty-nine years old. Lemaire was forty-six."

"Did she work in his department?" Nico asked.

"No, she had a job in intensive care."

"Was either one of them having trouble at the hospital?"

"None. Everybody knew that Lemaire and Janin were having an affair, but it didn't seem to bother anyone."

"And did either of them have problems in any other area of their lives?"

"Nothing that we can pin down for sure. Some people at the hospital suspected that Janin's wife's had finally learned about the affair. And he had hoped to receive the Ham-Wassermann prize from the American Hematology Society. A Chinese fellow from Ruijin Hospital, which is part of Shanghai Medical School, won the prize instead. He was very disappointed."

"How disappointed?"

"Professor Janin had slaved away in labs his entire life and had made significant contributions to the field. His work was recognized the world over. He had aspirations and even dreamed of winning the Nobel Prize one day."

"What about Danièle Lemaire?"

"She was in love. She would have given him anything."

"Even her life?"

"That's what people said."

"Did they know Christophe Parize?" Nico asked.

"Professor Janin and Dr. Parize were very close. They had lunch together often. Parize had great respect for Janin, who was something of a mentor, and Janin used Parize to widen his sphere of influence."

Nico noted that there was a fifteen-year age difference between Janin and Parize. Michel Cohen and he had a similar age span. Nico could understand the relationship.

Becker interrupted. "Both had experienced professional disappointments and were going through rough patches at home. And they were thick as thieves."

"But to give up everything together?" Nico said.

His phone rang. It was his secretary. "Professor Vilars would like to talk to you."

"I'll take it, thanks." He heard a click.

"Nico? I just finished the autopsy and let Charlotte Maurin and the crime scene investigator go. I imagine you can't wait to know my conclusions."

"Magistrate Becker and Commander Kriven are in my office. I'm putting you on speakerphone, if that's okay with you."

"Perfect, two birds with one stone: the police and the court."

"Go ahead. Everyone is listening."

"I'll try to be brief. I have confirmed that the body was that of Christophe Parize, based on his size, weight, a scar on his upper-left arm, and his dental records. We'll have the DNA results tomorrow. After determining his identity, I focused on the drowning itself and the time spent in the water. The dribble found on his lips is foam. In a live submersion, the mixture of air, water, and mucus will appear around the mouth and nose two to three hours after the body is extracted and then disappear with decomposition. This was the case with our body. Furthermore, his lungs were full of water, which corroborates death from drowning. Finally, we found plant plankton and diatoms common to the Seine."

"Which means that Parize was drowned in the river," Nico said.

"That's correct. The body temperature and overall state leads us to conclude that the victim was in the water for thirty-six hours. The time of death is sometime between midnight and two on Saturday morning. In addition, the victim has a gash on his right wrist and forearm, most likely caused by rope. I also found a bluish gelatinous hematoma in his brain. I conclude that Christophe Parize was tied up and knocked out, which is confirmed by the epistaxis noted by the river patrol. Finally, the ear injury is unrelated to the cause of death. It's a postmortem tear inflicted by rats. I hope this gives you something to work with."

"It does. Thank you for doing this on such short notice."

"It's nothing. See you soon. I'm sure I will be, considering all the bodies you're piling on me these days."

She hung up. Armelle Vilars liked getting a little jab in. Nico knew it was friendly, her way of teasing him.

"At least things are clear," Becker said. "Dr. Parize was tied up and taken to the Île aux Cygnes, where he got hit behind the head and was sent off to dreamland. Then someone threw him from the pier into the water, tied to an anchor. A harsh way to wake up. And all of that just a few hours after our fake Dr. Parize was exhumed. Another coincidence."

"What will the prosecutor decide to do?"

"He'll give me the full investigation. We now have three murders on our hands. Obviously, we need to focus on Dr. Parize. He is key to the mystery. Once we know his story, we'll be able to solve the cases involving Bruno Guedj and the fellow in the car fire."

"I'm meeting with Christophe Parize's parents," Kriven said.

"I'll have his ex-wife and their children come to headquarters," Nico said. "It's time we had a little conversation with them in here."

"And we need to compare what Janin and Parize were working on," Becker said.

Kriven sighed. "We'll be at it for days."

"I'll ask Rost to put his three detective squads on it," Nico said. "That's eighteen people. We're on their heels, so let's get going and start biting at them."

Becker and Kriven nodded, looking determined. They all had the feeling that the hourglass had turned over. Their time was no longer running out, but the murderers' time was.

22

"What area or areas of medicine would involve both hemato-oncology and immunology?" Nico asked.

Caroline gave him a reflective look as she considered the question. That look had captivated him months ago, when he had met her in her office as a patient.

"Both specialties have a connection to blood cells, which play a key role in the respiratory and immune systems and in coagulation. Hematology is largely focused on the production and circulation of blood cells, which involve the bone marrow and lymphoid organs. A hemato-oncologist specializes in the various forms of cancers related to the discipline and their treatment. That is where the immunologist comes in. Immunology is a very broad field. In this case, the immunologist studies the interactions between the cancer cells and the immune system. It involves the recognition of cancer-specific antigens that trigger the immune response. The aim is finding one or more therapies that slow the progress of the disease. This area of immunology has been growing quite rapidly and has been responsible for the introduction of antibody therapies, vaccines, and tumor-marker diagnostic tests that have changed how cancer is treated and have increased survival rates for leukemia, myeloma, and lymphoma patients, as well as survival rates for those with solid tumors. But there's still a long way to go. Was that clear?"

"Perfectly. And now I have a riddle. A hemato-oncologist and an immunologist are competing in the X Games. Who has the better odds of winning?"

Caroline smiled. "The hemato-oncologist, because he can take his lumps."

"Right!" Nico said, kissing her hand.

Nico was sure of one thing: Christophe Parize and Claude Janin were not in the same league. The immunology professor was Nobel material. So if their disappearances had something to do with medicine, they needed to look at the mentor's research. It was in the area of T-cell lymphomas.

Once again, Nico called on Caroline for help.

"We have three types of cells: red blood cells, white blood cells or leucocytes, and platelets," she said. "There are also different types of leucocytes, including T cells, which play a key role in immunity. A number of diseases affect leucocytes, most notably lymphomas, and there are several types of T-cell lymphomas. Some are more common than others, and some strike children and young adults more often than people who are older. One form that children seem to get more often is lymphoblastic lymphoma. It spreads quickly. Tumors sometimes develop behind the breastbone and interfere with breathing. Frequently, both the bone marrow and the blood are affected, and this is called acute lymphoblastic T-cell leukemia. It is often quite aggressive."

"So what does an immunologist who's researching weapons to use against these bad guys do?"

"He identifies lymphoma antigens, produces antibodies, and does clinical trials."

"On animals?"

"Yes, before any therapy can be used on people, animal testing must be done. Years can go by between the first tests and patient trials."

"And where does chemotherapy fit into all of this?"

"It's a key part of the cancer-fighting arsenal. It kills cancerous cells and keeps them from proliferating. The protocol varies, depending on the lymphoma and the patient. It is often necessary to prescribe high doses of chemotherapy. Unfortunately, chemotherapy is very hard on the body. I hope it will become archaic one day. The kinds of targeted therapies that I mentioned before are the future of cancer treatment."

After giving all this some thought, Nico ordered Kriven, Théron, and Charlotte Maurin to come up with a list of T-cell lymphoma patients treated by Dr. Parize and to cull the patients who also had some connection to Professor Janin. This would narrow the scope of the investigation.

Meanwhile, the molar was making the headlines. Some editors had bought the practical-joke theory and were clamoring for stories about medical-school pranks. Some reporters, however, were taking a more serious tack and wanted to know where the division's investigation was going. Fortunately, none of them appeared to be aware of the connection between Bruno Guedj's alleged suicide and Christophe Parize's murder.

Nico had convinced the Guedj family to play along. But how long would they put up with this? The pharmacist's death was certainly no prank. Nico was more determined than ever to find out who murdered him.

The team had also let Dr. Maxime Robert and Maître Belin, Guedj's dentist and notary, in on the secret. Both were cooperative and eager to get to the bottom of the mystery.

The DNA test results had confirmed that it was the doctor who had been found in the water. The police forensics lab had also filed its report on the anchor used to weigh down the body. It was new and a popular brand, selling for a couple of thousand euros in most marine-supply stores. It weighed sixty-eight pounds and was designed for boats that were sixty-eight to 150 feet long. Nothing useful.

Nico glanced at the clock on the wall. Mrs. Parize and her two children would be arriving soon.

The day before, Kriven had questioned Parize's parents, who had traveled from Burgundy. The mother had broken down in tears when she learned that her beloved son's death in a car accident had been staged. She cried harder at the news of his real death. The father was in shock. Both were brokenhearted, crushed by their son's deception.

Nico's secretary called to let him know that the Parize family had been led to a tiny room on the top floor, which had only a small skylight. The sergeant accompanying them was supposed to be a ghost. That was police jargon: His job was to watch everything and be invisible, for all intents and purposes.

Nico took the staircase up to a long hallway lined with interview rooms. The sergeant saluted him before closing the door behind them.

Mrs. Parize and her two children jumped up from their chairs. They looked afraid. Nico felt bad about it, but he had decided to give them a clear message: he was serious. If one of them had key information about Parize, or if the doctor had contacted a family member, Nico wanted a confession.

"Sit down, please," he said.

"You summoned us," Mrs. Parize said.

"That's correct. I have some questions about Dr. Parize."

"I thought I answered them when you came to see me on Saturday."

Since then, things had changed.

"Christophe did not die in a car accident last year in Burgundy," he said without offering any cushion. He watched their reactions.

Marine turned pale and covered her mouth, muffling a cry. Her mother turned red. Nico figures she was feeling both afraid and angry. Olivier remained stoic and distant, a vague look in his eyes. Was it a wordless expression of hatred for his father?

"What do you mean?" Mrs. Parize finally asked.

"As you know, ma'am, we exhumed the body buried in Chalon-sur-Saône. The coroner did an autopsy and concluded that it wasn't your ex-husband."

"Are you sure?"

"Absolutely. Since the accident, has he tried to contact any of you?"

"No," Mrs. Parize cried out.

"Not even you, Miss Parize?" Nico looked Marine in the eye.

The young woman shook her head, still in shock.

"Your father was near the Lycée Louis-le-Grand on September 15, presumably to see you at the ceremony in your honor."

The girl's lips began to tremble.

"We think that he tried to approach you."

"We didn't see him. I didn't leave Marine's side the whole time," the brother said.

Nico sized him up.

"Then maybe you are the one he contacted?"

"Me? Never!" the boy yelled.

"Olivier!" his mother shouted.

The teenager looked down, clearly uncomfortable. "I'm sorry. Where is our father? And why did he lead us to believe he was dead? Did he do something bad?"

"Would that surprise you?"

"It's impossible," Marine whispered. Tears were rolling down her cheeks.

"It's true we fought a lot," the mother said. "The divorce was hard. But is that enough reason to disappear?"

"He wanted the department head position at Saint Louis Hospital. One of his colleagues got it instead."

"He must have been furious," Mrs. Parize said, obviously surprised by the news.

"That was his whole life."

"It could have been a reason to disappear."

She shrugged.

"At the end, he was in a bad mood all the time. Now I understand better," Olivier said.

"He didn't care about us anymore," Marine said.

"Except that he tried to see you on September 15," Nico pressed. "He was very proud of you."

"He had always been proud of Marine. He had reason to be," Oliver said. Nico didn't pick up any tinge of resentment in his tone.

"Stop. He was proud of you, too," Marine said softly.

"Okay, he was close to Marine," Nico said. "That's what motivated him to go to the reception. We have witnesses. So I'll ask again, Marine. Did he talk to you? If so, what did he tell you? It is extremely important. If you keep anything that serious from the police, you'll be in trouble."

"I swear I didn't see him," Marine said.

"She's not lying. Marine never lies," her protective brother said.

"Please, leave my children alone," Mrs. Parize interrupted. "We don't know anything."

"Does the name Bruno Guedj mean anything to you?"

"Guedj? No," the mother answered. "What about you, Marine and Olivier?"

"I don't know anyone named Bruno Guedj."

It was time to break the news.

"I have something to tell you, and it won't be easy to hear. Dr. Parize was found dead yesterday."

Oliver went pale and swayed in his chair.

"What happened?" Mrs. Parize shrieked.

"He drowned."

"Christophe knew how to swim!"

"Let's just say he had some help."

"Do you mean someone killed him?"

"That's correct. I'm sorry. Please accept my condolences."

"Dear God! How did this happen?"

"You'll have to tell me."

"We'd tell you if we knew anything," Oliver said. He was taking on the role of head of the family, with all the clumsiness and hesitation of his age.

"I certainly hope so, just like I hope you share my commitment to finding your father's murderer. You may go home now. I have no further questions."

They remained slumped in their chairs. Finally, they got up to leave. Many times before, Nico had seen how pain and sorrow sucked up their prey from the inside, emptying them of their substance, like straws in a glass.

Nico stopped Olivier at the door.

"Here's my card. If anything at all comes back to you, any detail, don't hesitate to call."

The young man was obviously shaken. He took the card and hurried to catch up with his sister and mother in the hallway. The ghost sergeant accompanied them. He had played his role brilliantly. Nico hadn't even noticed him.

Nico went back over the interview as he walked down to his office. A successful investigation required several ingredients: work, determination—more on the order of relentless resolve—intuition, and insight—a sixth sense, which no technique could ever replace. And luck, a basic element that couldn't be controlled. For example, Christophe Parize's body wouldn't have been found as quickly, had river patrol divers not decided to inspect the area. They would need more luck to figure out what

Bruno Guedj had in common with Dr. Parize, Professor Claude Janin, and the nurse, Danièle Lemaire. For that matter, what, other than what they already knew, linked Parize, Janin, and Lemaire? At this point, he didn't have anything that could explain the tragic series of events.

Nico put on his coat. He needed to empty his mind; this case was getting to him. He kept seeing the faces of Guedj's family members superimposed on those of Parize's family. Outside, he walked across the Pont Neuf. On the left bank of the Seine, he passed a cast-iron Wallace fountain, an icon of the French capital. At the end of the nineteenth century, British philanthropist Richard Wallace had decided to use part of his immense fortune to benefit the needy of Paris. At the time, water was more precious than wine. Wallace commissioned fifty drinking fountains, which were to be beautiful, as well as functional. Four nymphs on the pedestal of each represented simplicity, kindness, charity, and sobriety. The Samaritan now lay in the Père Lachaise Cemetery.

On the Quai des Grands Augustins, booksellers were hawking their antique and used wares. The *bouquinistes* and their green boxes were another symbol of Paris. At one of the stands, he and Caroline had unearthed a Surrealistic drawing of the capital, which they framed and hung at his place. Now, every time he saw it, he recalled that moment spent strolling along the Seine. It seemed impossible to remember a certain scene without also remembering the loved one who shared the experience. Was it because the loved one made the scene all the more beautiful?

He pushed open the door to the travel agency.

23

Who did that cop think he was? That Sirsky. Some puffed-up idiot making his intentions clear by telling the world that Bruno Guedj's death was a practical joke. Did Sirsky think he was an imbecile? Did he really think those headlines would goad him into revealing himself? Dumb cop. Asshole. He was a nobody who had the gall to play with the big boys.

But in this chess game, he didn't really care if, in the end, his king lay down. That made it all the more dangerous. He was sure he could kill the bishops and rooks before laying down his weapon. With .22-caliber long-rifle bullets.

And when he fell, his last gaze would be on his queen, who had chosen to sell her soul to the devil, and his, along with it.

24

"Hello? Chief Sirsky?" The voice was hesitant.

Nico searched his memory. He knew that voice. "Yes, it's me."

"I'd like to see you. Can I?" The words barely came out.

"Of course."

"At the Place Saint-Michel?" The young man sounded relieved. "It's near your office."

"When?"

"Right away?"

"I'll be there in five minutes."

The kid had chosen a busy café with lots of people milling about. What was he afraid of?

Nico walked purposefully without hurrying. He wanted to look strong and calm, to bring the student out of his shell and gain his trust. This meeting was the first good news they had gotten in two days. His team was moving heaven and earth at Saint Louis Hospital but had yet to find a crack in the system. Maybe this was the break they needed.

Nico entered the café, scanned the customers, and headed toward the table.

"Sirs?" a waiter asked.

"Hot chocolate for me," Nico said, trying to sound relaxed. "What would you like?"

"The same."

Nico could have ordered anything, and the young man would have done the same. He had something on his mind.

"Two hot chocolates," the waiter yelled and walked away.

"You wanted to see me?" Nico made sure his tone was friendly.

"Yes—" He hesitated.

"Is it about your father?"

Olivier Parize nodded. He was nineteen. Nearly a man, but not quite. His whole life was in front of him, offering both opportunities and difficult decisions. Dimitri in just five years!

The waiter reappeared with a platter balanced on his fingertips. He set the steaming cups in front of them, along with the bill. Nico grabbed the slip.

"My father left an envelope for me at school."

"When was that?"

"Ten days ago."

"Well before our conversation!"

"What was in it scared me to death."

Now Nico understood Olivier Parize's attitude when he was questioned. He had defended his sister fiercely, sure that she didn't know anything, because he was the one his father had chosen to warn. Oliver had been petrified when he heard that his father was murdered.

The boy opened his backpack and handed over the letter.

My dear son Olivier,

I know I hurt you and your sister, and I'm going to hurt you some more. With this letter, you will know that I did not die in that car accident last year. Blinded by the problems with your mother and trouble at the hospital, I chose to disappear from your lives when the opportunity arose. It

was totally crazy, and I regret it bitterly. Like
the day I slapped you. You didn't deserve it. But
we can never go back. If you find out that I am
dead—for real this time—it will mean that I've
been murdered, and the person responsible for my
death has lost all sense of reality. In that case, and
only in that case, give this letter to the police, and
tell them that I am sorry for Bruno Guedj. I know
it doesn't look that way, but I love you, and I love
Marine, too. I didn't show you my love the way I
should have, and I am paying for it now.—Papa.

"Are you sure it's from him?"

"He talks about the slap."

"What slap?"

"We were supposed to go on a vacation together, but
he called it off. We had a fight, and he slapped me. Then,
a few days later, he had his car accident."

"Was there anything with the letter?"

Olivier Parize slipped his hand into his backpack and
pulled out a glossy photo.

"It's a class picture. That's Marine, her junior year in
high school at Louis-le-Grand."

Nothing was written on the back.

"Do you have any idea what it could mean?"

"No."

"Did you talk to your sister?"

"Last night."

"I need to see her."

The boy pulled out his cell phone and made the call.
"She's on her way."

"Where is she?"

"In the café across the street. I figured you'd want to
see her."

Nico didn't say anything until the girl had joined them. She looked frail and tired. It was hard to imagine her as head of her class at such a prestigious school.

"Who are these other teenagers in the photo?"

"Former classmates."

"They are not in your class anymore?"

"Some continued on after graduation, like I did, but others went elsewhere."

"Your father is using this picture to tell us something. What could it be?"

"We don't have the slightest idea," Oliver said. "We were up all night. We thought you might have an idea."

"Can you give me their names?"

"Of course, we spent three years together."

Nico took out a notebook and pen and wrote down a number for each face. He flashed back to the number 510 on Bruno Guedj's decapitated head and shivered.

Marine listed the identities of all thirty-eight students. Nico asked questions about their parents' professions, their status in school, their plans for the future, and any problems she might have known about. He was pulling at straws, and she provided all the answers that she could. Little by little, the girl relaxed and started to say more. Occasionally, her brother had something to add.

"She started getting really, really sick. It was terrible. My father took care of her at the hospital," Marine said.

Nico stopped writing and looked up. "Excuse me, what is her name again?"

"It's Clarisse Quere," Marine said.

Nico rubbed his chin. "Quere. As in Edward Quere?"

"Yes."

"*The* Edward Quere? The billionaire?"

"The third-richest man in France," Olivier said.

"What did she have?"

"It was serious," Marine said. "Cancer."

"So your father cared for her. Why him?"

"Our parents knew each other from meetings and other events at school. Mr. Quere called Dad, I think."

"Do you remember when this was?"

"Clarisse got sick at the beginning of the school year. I think it was November."

"How is she today?"

Marine's eyes filled with tears. "I don't know. At first, she kept a blog. We had news. Sometimes I'd talk with her on the phone. Then, all of a sudden, she stopped communicating."

"Did your father talk to you about her?"

"Dad told me I should keep my hopes up."

"That had to be hard."

"You were very upset," Oliver said. "You wanted to stay in touch with her, to let her know that you cared. When she stopped posting on her blog, you started getting really worried."

"Exactly when did that happen?" Nico asked.

"In July."

"A month before his car accident," Nico said.

"Yes, that's it."

"Do you think that's an important detail?" Olivier asked.

"Perhaps. We'll see. Let's keep going with these names, please. There are a few more faces left."

They finished putting names on the faces, and it was clear that the only student of real interest was Clarisse Quere.

"I want to say something," Olivier said.

Nico looked him in the eye. The boy's lips were trembling.

"My sister and my mother knew nothing about the letter. If there is someone to blame for withholding evidence, it's me."

"Let's just say that for now, I don't intend to blame anyone."

"You're not going to arrest me?"

"I'd rather lock up your father's murderers."

"Do you think we are in danger?" Marine asked, alarmed.

"No. Whatever your father did had nothing to do with you. And you haven't had any contact with him in months."

"Okay, and will the letter he gave Olivier help you understand what happened?"

"It's too early to tell."

"But you're interested in Clarisse Quere, right?"

"It's a lead, but you must not say a word about it, under any circumstances. That could cause troubles for you."

"Mum's the word," Olivier said.

The two looked relieved of a heavy weight. Oliver had gotten his father's letter off his conscience. But the two of them still seemed nervous and tense. Nico felt for them. Losing a father was bad enough. Losing a father in such an inconceivable and intolerable way was even worse.

Nico tried to calm his excitement as he crossed the Saint Michel Bridge and headed back to police headquarters. The Parize children had just provided them with a prime lead, saving the division a lot of time. His teams probably would have found the connection eventually, but how many hours would they have spent looking through patient files at Saint Louis Hospital? And how would they have known that Clarisse Quere's case was different? They would have needed to know that the girl was in Marine Parize's class, a detail that wouldn't have shown up anywhere.

Claire Le Marec stopped him in the hallway. "You okay?"

He started. He was so absorbed in thought, he didn't realize he was already at headquarters.

"I've got something," Nico said. "Call everyone into my office right now."

She nodded and headed off to gather the troops. Nico had to force himself to quiet his nerves. He was that excited.

Three minutes later, Jean-Marie Rost was in front of him, champing at the bit. "So?"

"I just saw Olivier Parize. He called me. Ten days ago, he received a letter from his father. It was intended for us, in case he got killed."

"He knew his father was alive?" Kriven asked.

"Not until then." Nico took the letter out of the envelope and tossed it on his desk, along with the photo.

"Well, I'll be damned," Kriven said after reading the letter. "Parize makes a clear connection between Guedj's fate and his own."

"And it was his turn to fear for his life," Rost said. "He's accusing some mysterious man behind the scenes. He sounds angry."

"What's this picture about?" Le Marec asked.

"It's Marine's junior-year class. She's there," Nico said.

Everyone leaned in to get a closer look at the glossy.

"Now look at this girl. She's our lead in the case. Clarisse Quere, daughter of Edward."

"High society." Kriven let out a whistle.

"Clarisse Quere developed a serious illness. Guess who her doctor was."

"Christophe Parize," Rost said.

"Exactly."

Everyone fell silent.

"Parize knew we'd make the connection with Clarisse Quere if he got this picture to us," Kriven finally said. "Now we have something to go on: the Quere family. This is big."

"But we don't know what role the family plays," Le Marec said. "Maybe they're victims."

"We need to collect as much information as possible. We can't confront them without knowing what we're doing," Nico said, grabbing the telephone to call Magistrate Becker.

"Well, well," Becker said when he heard the news. "This could explode in our faces at any time. Before we approach the Quere family, we had better be well armed. First, we need to find out about Clarisse Quere's treatment at Saint Louis Hospital and the current state of her health. Let's see if we can connect Professor Janin to any of this."

"At the same time, I suggest that we look into Edward Quere," Nico said. "Let's find out more about him and his business dealings, especially what he's been up to lately."

"Is there anything else that we need to be doing?" Becker asked.

"Yes, get Bastien Gamby to find Clarisse's blog."

"You're going with Milgram, right?"

According to social psychologist Stanley Milgram, human society was really a small world in which people were connected by what he called short path lengths. In 1967, his small-world experiment led to the development of a significant theory: six degrees of separation. He held that two randomly chosen people were linked by an average of six people. Later studies explored this phenomenon online. They confirmed that five to seven degrees of separation were enough to connect one user to another. That meant that Bastien Gamby was never very far from the person he was tracking—most often a perverted vulture avid for human blood.

"If Clarisse Quere is still alive—if she isn't, we would have seen it in the papers—and if she still has enough strength to use a keyboard, then Bastien will find her, and he could connect with her."

25

"Consider yourself warned," Kriven said a few hours later. "There's nothing bright and cheery in Clarisse Quere's medical records."

They heard a knock at the door, and Le Marec stuck her head in.

"Come in," Nico said. "I was just getting an update."

"It's a simple story to begin with," Kriven said. "A little more than two years ago, Clarisse Quere sees her family doctor for a persistent cough. The doctor prescribes a treatment that doesn't work. Then Clarisse develops night sweats and chest pain. She goes to see her doctor a couple more times before he begins to take it a little more seriously. He orders a chest X-ray, thinking it's a lung infection, maybe pneumonia. What they discover is a fifteen-centimeter tumor in the mediastinum."

"What's that?" Le Marec asked.

"The thoracic region between the two lungs."

"Fifteen centimeters? And it went undetected?" Nico asked.

"In young people, tumors can go a long time without being detected. Kids are generally in pretty good health. They're tough. Until that point, Clarisse Quere was in good shape. She was a tennis champion. Once the tumor was identified, things sped up. The doctor and Clarisse's father contacted Dr. Parize. As you know, he had a daughter in Clarisse's class. Parize took over the case at the hospital. The girl spent a week there getting all the needed tests and exams. They did a mediastinoscopy to get a sample of the tumor. Then they did a scan of her chest, abdomen, and pelvis, followed by a bone marrow biopsy and a lumbar tap. The results were a bombshell: T-cell lymphoblastic lymphoma."

"Poor girl," Le Marec said.

"There was good news, though: the tumor hadn't spread. Clarisse and her parents signed on for the treatment protocol, and she underwent two months of chemotherapy. But the tumor didn't shrink enough. She then entered the second phase: an autologous bone marrow transplant. Stem cells from the patient are harvested and stored before the start of an intensive chemotherapy regimen. In effect, it's Hiroshima in the human body. Once the blast is over, the stem cells are returned to the patient's body, so blood cells can be manufactured again. The patient is then kept in a sterile room for ten days to two weeks so the cells can multiply.

"After all of that, Clarisse was able to leave the hospital. She got better. The family was relieved to see her get back to her normal life. All of which brings us to the following spring."

"Are we to conclude that Clarisse Quere was cured?" Nico asked.

"At the time, that's what everyone hoped."

"But she relapsed, didn't she?" Le Marec said.

"That's right. One morning, when she was washing up, she noticed that the glands in her neck were swollen. A biopsy confirmed the return of her T-cell lymphoblastic lymphoma."

"What did Dr. Parize decide to do?" Nico asked.

"A multidisciplinary meeting was called, with several doctors from the unit, along with a radiotherapist and a grafter. They discussed the possibility of an allogeniec bone marrow transplant—a transplant from another donor. But there were two major problems: Clarisse had no suitable donors in her family, and she had a heart problem."

"She had cardiac problems too?" Le Marec said.

"Not at first, but between the disease and the chemo, her heart was weakened."

"If she was going to die anyway, why not try to operate?" Le Marec said.

"Doctors have a fundamental principle: the treatment must not kill the patient. And here, the risk was huge. Dr. Parize broke the news to Edward Quere."

"And that's all? That's how it ended?" Le Marec was clearly feeling frustrated.

"They suggested more chemo to slow the progression of the disease and buy a little time. It was the end of July, a month before Parize's accident."

"How much time did they give Clarisse?" Nico asked.

"Six months to a year. The head of the hematology-oncology department told us that in a similar case, she advised the parents to take their son on a trip somewhere wonderful, a place where they could enjoy their last months together. Well, the parents removed their son from Saint Louis Hospital and found a new doctor who admitted him to another hospital, where he died, not in the arms of his parents but on tubes and monitors. She swore she would never advise that again. It's a rare parent who can accept the inevitability of a child's death. Most will fight it to the end."

"How did Edward Quere react?"

"It broke him. She was his only child. At the beginning of September, he signed her release forms, and the hospital never saw Clarisse again."

"Did you find any connection between Quere and Professor Janin?"

"Following the mediastinoscopy, Professor Janin got authorization to remove a sample of the tumor for his T-cell lymphoma studies. He was conducting some very promising research. Janin and Edward Quere were seen together at the hospital. But Quere wasn't just anybody, and he knew Parize, so there was nothing strange about Janin meeting with Quere to discuss his research."

"And the girl? Did she die?"

"Apparently not," Kriven said. "We didn't find any death certificate."

"Did you mention Clarisse's blog?"

"The department head told us that many young people with health conditions have interactive diaries. It's a way to share their feelings and views, and it can be very important if the teen is isolated from schoolmates and other friends. Also, they use online discussion groups to learn about their diseases and possible treatments. Kids are clever. As much as their parents and doctors try to filter the information they get, they'll always find someone online who will tell them what they want to know."

"We'll come back to that later, but first, let's talk about Clarisse, and particularly her father, Edward Quere."

"Maurin's team was on that," Rost said. "Here's a summary of the main points. Edward Quere just celebrated his fifty-first birthday. He was born in Lille and attended elite schools. After that, he joined his father's civil engineering firm, which, under his command, became a leading company in the field. He sold it at a considerable profit. From there, Quere became a takeover specialist. He bought out troubled companies, propped them up, and sold them off, again, at quite a profit. Today, he's invested in haute couture, leather goods, and cosmetics. He runs several department stores and owns a major financial newspaper. On the private side, he loves tennis and art. He is married. His only child is Clarisse, whom the couple had trouble conceiving, so it seems. When Clarisse got into the Lycée Louis-le-Grand, Quere decided he would begin grooming her to take over his empire. Her illness has apparently shattered his dream.

Clarisse left school during her junior year. She is eighteen and hasn't even graduated from high school."

"What a shame," Le Marec said.

"And her mother?"

"She seems to lead a quiet life. She restored paintings before she married Quere, but stopped working after the wedding."

"In early September of last year, Quere took his daughter out of Saint Louis Hospital. Where is she now?" Nico asked.

"There is no trace of Clarisse Quere in the Paris public hospital system," Kriven answered. "None in Lille, where her father grew up, either. To make it tougher, there is no record of her in the state health-insurance system. Of course, she could be in a private clinic in Europe or the United States. Quere could afford to send his daughter anywhere."

The room went silent as they considered the pieces of the puzzle. First, there was Edward Quere's daughter, who had incurable cancer. Quere would have been willing to do anything to save his child's life. Then there was Dr. Parize, who had passed along a letter and one of his daughter's class pictures to suggest the mess he had gotten into. A secretary had recognized Parize at the school when he had dropped off the envelope containing the letter and the photo. He had stressed the importance of his son getting that envelope. Why had he been willing to expose himself again? Was it because his first encounter in public—the one with Bruno Guedj—had put him on a blacklist? His employer Edward Quere's blacklist?

"I'll call Bastien," Nico said, breaking the silence.

The cybercop was there in a minute, looking, as usual, as though he belonged in another world.

"I went through Clarisse's blog. She sure had it rough," he said as he tossed a pack of printouts on the table. "There's a lot more, but here's some of it."

Le Marec began reading aloud.

Clarisse: Hi. My name is Clarisse, and I'm sixteen
years old. Two months ago, I began to cough. It
got worse, and my doctor sent me for X-rays. They
found a mass in my chest. My father took me
to see a specialist, a friend's father, which made
me feel better. I have a bunch of tests to take.
Nobody tells me anything. I'm afraid it might
be serious, and I can't sleep. My mother seems
so sad, even though she tries not to show it. My
father tells me to be strong. But I'm very scared.

Pilou56: Hi, Clarisse. Lots of things in life
blow up in our faces. That's why we need
to live to the fullest every second. Maybe
it's not so serious after all. Don't get worked
up so quickly. Keep us posted. Hugs.

JuJu: A year ago, everything was going great in my
life—friends, family, work. Then a lump appeared
on my clavicle. It ended up being lymph-node
cancer: Hodgkin's disease. Chemo, radiotherapy,
the works. After months of anxiety, I'm starting
to feel better and get back to my normal life.
You have to fight, and you can beat the disease.
I'm LIVING proof. Good luck, Clarisse. BTW,
I'm twenty-three and going to be an uncle.

Clarisse: It was a hard week. Thanks to all of
you for your support. It made me feel better.
The news is not good. I've got leukemia. I'm
starting two months of chemo. Seeing the
faces my parents are pulling, it must be serious.
Does anybody know anything about this?

LLG-juniors: We're with you, Clarisse. Come back soon. In two months? Big sloppy kisses.

Ocean2000: Isn't it better to know what you're fighting? You talked about a mass in your chest, and now leukemia. I'd bet on a lymphoma. There are different kinds, and they are more or less aggressive. Two months of chemo is rough. It'll make you tired and nauseous. You'll throw up, lose your hair, and have diarrhea. Hold tight.

Clarisse: High-grade T-cell lymphoblastic mediastinal lymphoma. That's Chinese to me. It's my third chemo session, and I'm beat. I'm trying to stay hopeful. It's not easy. I just want to get better and go back to school.

DrNo: Acute lymphoblastic leukemia = ALL. The prognosis can depend on your risk of relapse (which increases over the age of thirty-five, so that's one point in your favor), your white blood-cell count, and your ALL subtype.

Lol: DrNo gets right to the point, doesn't he? Maybe he's a real doc? In any case, James Bond wins in the end. I guess you're not in the best shape, darling. But keep fighting; you'll be okay. Rely on your support system. That counts for a lot. I know. My son's been there.

Clarisse: I'd be interested in knowing what your son had, Lol. I hope with all my heart that he's still around. Me, I've hit rock bottom. The assessment wasn't so good. My lymphoma is partially resistant. I need what they call an autologous bone marrow transplant. I had so many plans. I wanted to finish school, go work with my father, find a husband, have kids, be happy. I want to believe it's still possible.

Lol: He got it when he was twenty and in medical school. I'm not making that up. He had a sore throat and was tired. It was late-stage large B-cell mediastinal lymphoma. We're lucky, and he came through. It's behind us now. So I understand what you're going through, and I'm with you and your parents.

Clarisse: I'm out of the hospital. Every day, I feel a little better. Life is wonderful. I'll be able to go back to school in the fall, and soon I'll be playing tennis again. I'll be a year behind, but what does that matter? It's almost sum-mer, and my father is taking the whole month of August off to take us on a trip. I'm happy again. Thanks to all of you. Without you…

Bella: Congratulations! You beat cancer. Live long!

Clarisse: My God, I'm scared. Everything was go-ing so well. I was supposed to get on a plane in two weeks to go to the United States with my parents—San Francisco, Los Angeles, Las Vegas, New York. A dream trip. But yesterday, the glands in my neck felt swollen. They didn't hurt, but I thought they were a little big. I showed my mom. She called Dad right away, and he raced home. That's not normal. My dad is very busy and has lots of responsibilities. He wouldn't have come for nothing. He drove me to the hospital, and it all started again. I have a biopsy tomorrow. The doctors are worried about a relapse. It sucks. I'm furious, and I can't stop crying.

NatachaBordeaux: I'm totally moved. My mother had liver cancer. She got better for eight years, and we thought she was cured. Then it started again. I'm afraid she's going to die. She's so, so wonderful.

Lol: Post news as soon as you know. I'm sending lots of positive energy.

Clarisse: Lymphoma, the return. I'm in the hospital. Good thing I've got my laptop to keep chatting with you. The bigwigs are meeting tomorrow to talk about my case. I want to throw up just thinking about chemo. My mother left. I think she needs to cry and doesn't want me to see her doing that. My father's harder, like ice. I understand. He'd do the impossible for me, but there's nothing he can do. We'll see what tomorrow brings.

Lol: Don't give up, dear Clarisse. Don't let the disease win. I know you've got the strength deep inside.

Clarisse: You're right, Lol. Thanks. But I'm so scared.

DrNo: Dammit, fight! Man up. Volley, slice, smash, lob. Give it everything you have, just like tennis.

StrawberrySyrup: You're gonna win this match. Don't lose it on the bench.

Superman: Beat the lympho- ma, because you're worth it.

Clarisse: Sorry to disappoint you, but it's over. I lost the match. The doctors can't do anything.

I'm alone. My father left the hospital. He said
he needed to think. About what? He can return
those plane tickets to the US. We won't ever
use them. You know what? I kissed a boy once.
On the cheek. It was in fourth grade. I would
have loved knowing what it's like to kiss on the
lips… To love someone. Now I'll never know.

Kokillette: I'm thinking of you.

Clarisse: Dad came to get me. I won't be
going back to the hospital. He promised. He
says there is still hope. One day we'll go to
the US, like we planned. He's the best dad.

Le Marec looked up. Her colleagues were all still.
"And here we are," Nico said finally.

26

The irony of life. He would have laughed about it, but the moans he heard felt like daggers in his heart. He would have given anything to be the one lying on that bed, twisting in pain, breathing his last breaths. In her place. If only going into forbidden territory, playing apprentice sorcerer, and spilling blood had been enough. Fate was horrifying. How could you fight it? You couldn't. You had to accept it. No fortune or power could change that. Everyone was equal in the face of death. How nauseating.

The sound of clinking flasks made him jump. What good would it do to continue?

"We've made progress, great progress," a deep voice said.

It was nothing but a farce.

27

It was Friday. It had been a month since Bruno Guedj's murder and the arrival of his body in Marcel's cold room. An anniversary. Three sharp knocks at the door put an end to Alexandre Becker and Nico Sirsky's reflection. A secretary led Dr. Christine Sahian into the magistrate's office. The two men stood up and shook her hand.

The doctor looked incredulous, as if she still couldn't believe that she had been summoned to the courthouse. The two men had chosen to have the meeting on their turf, obliging the woman to play by their rules. Without her white coat, she had lost just a bit of the stature that went with her position. Dr. Sahian ran the Hematology-Oncology Department at Saint Louis Hospital, and her statement would be pure gold.

"I'm having trouble understanding what you want from me," she said in a tone that Nico imagined she used on recalcitrant patients.

She was thin, almost skinny. She wore her long brown hair in a ponytail. Her dark eyes had an untamed look. Despite the rigors of her job, the strength of character she needed to do it, and her maturity—Nico thought she had to be in her forties—she came off as almost childish. Faded jeans and a turtleneck underscored that impression.

"Sit down," Magistrate Becker said, ignoring the remark.

"I don't need to tell you that my department is in shambles. The mystery and your investigation surrounding the death of our colleague, Dr. Parize, is taking its toll on all of us."

"We understand," Becker said. "But this is a criminal investigation, and you, too, must understand what is at stake. I assure you that we want this to be over as much as you do."

Dr. Sahian sighed. "You seem to be advancing a theory that is, well, inconceivable."

"Inconceivable for doctors who have integrity and keep the Hippocratic Oath," the judge replied.

"An oath doctors take to relieve suffering," Nico said, trying to provoke her.

"Indeed, but we also swear that we will not do anything that exceeds our capabilities," she said.

Nico was seated next to Dr. Sahian in front of Becker's desk. He leaned forward in his chair and turned his side to the magistrate so that he could face the doctor. Putting his elbow on the desk and his chin in his hand, he stared at her. Staging. Dr. Sahian gave a nearly imperceptible shiver.

"The line separating good and evil blurs on occasion," Nico said. "We see that all the time in our jobs. Some people cross the line despite themselves. Dr. Parize held the whole world responsible for not being named department head. You stole his spotlight."

"His private problems had destabilized him for several months. The board didn't think it was a good time to give him the responsibility," Sahian said, looking ill at ease.

"You just confirmed that Christophe Parize was going through a bad patch," Becker said. "Sometimes that's all it takes to make a bad decision, to get pulled to the dark side."

Nico held out the letter that Parize had written to his son. The woman reached for it. She licked her lips, a gesture that betrayed her anxiety. She read the letter attentively. Nico heard her curse under her breath. Her face paled.

"Allow me to summarize," Nico said. "A sixteen- or seventeen-year-old girl is treated in your department for late-stage lymphoblastic lymphoma, a worst-case scenario, with chemotherapy, a bone marrow transplant, and relapse. There is no hope. The teen is given a death sentence. And that's where things go wrong. The father is rich and powerful, and he decides to take her out of the hospital. He cannot accept watching her die. In secret, he gathers doctors capable of finding an innovative alternative solution and testing it on his daughter. What do you think?"

"It's impossible and entirely illegal!" the doctor shouted.

But her final ramparts were tumbling, and Nico jumped on the opportunity to push her. "Exactly our point. What specialists would that good father hire to get what he wanted?"

"You think Edward Quere put this scheme together, don't you? It's completely crazy," the woman insisted.

"We are just asking for your insight, were that to be the case," Becker said.

The two men stopped talking, letting her do battle with her conscience.

"He would need an immunologist," she finally said. "A lymphocyte specialist."

"A man like Professor Janin?" Nico asked.

"He has the right profile, doesn't he?" Becker added.

"Yes, he would have been an excellent choice, but you forget that he was lost at sea."

"That's another subject. Who else?" Nico continued to press her.

"He would also need a doctor who worked in a biotechnology lab and had the equipment necessary to create the right antibodies."

"That doctor would still need to be at his job?"

"Absolutely."

"Who else?" Becker asked.

"A hematologist to inject the antibodies and follow the patient step-by-step."

"Such as Christopher Parize?"

"In effect."

"In such a professional configuration, who would be the team leader?" Becker asked.

"The immunologist. He's the only one who could steer the whole thing, but in an endeavor such as this, he would have to be on the cutting edge of clinical research."

"Can you think of anyone else who would be part of the team?"

"A nurse for daily care, monitoring, and blood tests."

"Such as Danièle Lemaire?"

"Dear God! What are you imagining?"

"The unimaginable, doctor," Nico said.

Nico and Becker concluded the meeting with small talk to relieve the pressure and make the doctor feel better. She was very sorry that she hadn't discerned just how stressed Christophe Parize was. But his attacks and aggressiveness had made it impossible to feel any compassion for him. And that was probably what he needed the most.

After she left, Becker turned to Nico. "I know perfectly well what you have in mind. Have you thought out the consequences?"

"I know what I have to do," Nico responded, sounding much calmer than he actually was.

"I can't give you a warrant. You realize that, don't you? We have nothing but circumstantial evidence, nothing solid. All he'd have to do is make one phone call, and his lawyers would drag me through the mud."

"I understand. You don't have to justify yourself."

"So what are you going to do?"

"Engage in hand-to-hand combat. It should be sweet, as Dimitri would say."

Nicole Monthalet challenged him with her look. "Do you know what you're walking into?"

"I am perfectly aware of that, Commissioner," Nico said.

"Edward Quere! What next? The president of France?"

"If necessary, ma'am, yes."

"You've got some nerve, Chief Sirsky," she said, smiling.

"And lots of doubts every day, but that's not going to get us anywhere, is it?"

"I get the feeling you're ready for anything."

"I just want to have a conversation with him. A simple conversation."

"I don't believe that for a minute, Sirsky! You're going to provoke him, because Magistrate Becker cannot sign a warrant. Quere's cohort of lawyers would fight it. There's no evidence. What the daughter wrote online would carry no weight at all."

"Exactly, but I'm sure he's behind this whole thing."

"Was Bastien Gamby able to contact Clarisse and get some information out of her?"

"She's nowhere to be found. Gamby thinks they cut her means of communication off—too dangerous."

"That would make sense. Quere is far from stupid, or he wouldn't be where he is."

"His daughter is going to die. He wouldn't hesitate to buy God's services in person."

"Well, he went to the wrong counter. He's paying the devil."

Nico nodded, and Commissioner Monthalet picked up her telephone. "The police prefect, please," she told her secretary. She pushed the speakerphone button.

"Commissioner, it's always a pleasure to talk to you. What can I do for you?"

"I'm calling about the molar mystery, sir."

"Hmm. The newspapers are having a field day with it. And the story's bound to get bigger once everything gets out. I expect the Criminal Investigation Division to control all aspects of the investigation."

"That is the reason for my call, sir."

"I'm listening."

"My team needs to meet with Edward Quere."

"You're joking. Edward Quere? He's a friend of the president."

"Which does not put him above the law," Monthalet said.

"I didn't suggest that. I'll be damned. This case could cost me my job. It's worse than the jewelry heist. Who would have thought?"

"Life is full of surprises."

Nico gulped, and the commissioner winked at him. It was a close game. He admired this woman. She had a lot to lose.

"I suppose the magistrate has agreed to look the other way, as long as there isn't a fuss?" the prefect said.

"That about sums it up. If we want our investigation to move forward, we've got to do it."

"Commissioner, I don't know how you come by your powers of persuasion, but I can't seem to refuse you anything."

She smiled at Nico, and the tension drained from his shoulders.

"And remind Sirsky that he's not untouchable," the prefect grumbled. "Tell him this: 'Even on the highest throne in the world, you're still sitting on your ass.' That's Michel de Montaigne. He'll appreciate it."

"I'll do that, sir."

He hung up.

"We have the prefect's blessing, but don't let this come back to bite me, Sirsky."

28

Situated between the Place Vendôme and the Opéra Garnier, the Rue de la Paix was the most expensive real estate on the French Monopoly board. Paris's Boardwalk. As Nico parked his car, Commissioner Monthalet's words bounced in his head, along with a song by Zazie that Dimitri was always singing. Lots of drumming.

Nico shivered. Was it from the outside temperature or the glacial chill deep inside him? How far would he go to save his son?

Kriven pressed the doorbell. A man wearing an impeccable black suit and polished shoes answered the door.

"I'm Chief Sirsky of the Criminal Investigation Division. This is Detective Kriven. We're here to see Mr. Quere."

"May I see your badges?"

It wasn't a question. It was an expectation. The two detectives obliged.

"Are you armed?"

A second person appeared. He was scowling. Nico and Kriven looked at each other.

"We don't have to answer that question. Show us to Mr. Quere," Nico said tersely. They were off to a bad start.

"I regret, but Mr. Quere is absent at the moment."

Nico looked the butler straight in the eye, then pulled out a card and handed it to the man. "Please tell him we stopped by."

The door had closed on them, and Nico and Kriven stood there for a moment.

"My gut says he's here and just doesn't want to see us," Kriven said.

"I agree, with more than my gut. Look, his car is parked on the street. And I'd say that's his chauffeur right there waiting for him."

Nico and Kriven headed back to their vehicle. "Let's take a ride around the block and get ready to follow. You drive," Nico said.

Five minutes later, a well-dressed man left the house, followed by two men dressed in black.

"Keep a safe distance," Nico said.

Kriven knew the drill and eased away from the curb to follow the black Mercedes with tinted windows. As Nico focused on the car, he felt his pulse quicken.

"Damn it, they're stepping on it," Nico said.

"They've made us, Chief." Kriven picked up speed, swerved to the left to pass a Peugeot, and veered back to the right lane to keep the Mercedes in view.

"Watch out," Nico said.

A delivery truck pulled out of an alley, nearly hitting them. Kriven slammed on the brakes. Nico saw Quere's car turn right several blocks farther along and disappear.

"We lost them," Kriven said.

Nico pulled out his phone and dialed headquarters. "Claire, what do we know about Quere's properties?"

"We've got the list here. It's pretty long."

"Narrow it down to Paris and the surrounding area. Anything pop out at you?"

"Still long. Wait, we've got a residence in Marnes-la-Coquette, where neighbors reported some suspicious activity."

"What kind of suspicious activity?"

"A lot of trucks going in and out. Disturbing the peace. It's usually a very quiet residential neighborhood, I guess."

"That's it. Give me the address. And send a team."

As they sped toward the posh west Paris suburb, Nico called Becker.

"I don't have enough to get you in," Becker said. "You'll have to be diplomatic."

"Diplomatic, my ass. His goons lied to me, and then he took off."

"I can't issue a search warrant for a wounded ego, my friend. But I'm sure you'll find a way."

It was only a six-mile drive from Quere's home in Paris to his property in Marne-la-Coquette, but they hit traffic and it seemed to take forever. Nico could barely contain his impatience.

"We've got him now. I can feel it," he said, checking his gun, hoping he wouldn't need it.

Kriven could feel his boss's determination and didn't say anything. He knew he could trust Nico's instinct. He was ready.

They stopped in front of the monumental wrought-iron gates leading to the Queres' luxurious mansion. A millstone wall topped with closed-circuit cameras protected the villa. So much for the calm neighborhood. Kriven pulled up, and the gates opened before he had a chance to ring the buzzer. He started down the driveway lined with skeletal trees, the gates closing behind them. There was no one in sight. They pulled up to the house. The door to a glass-enclosed vestibule was open.

"I don't like this," Kriven said, getting out of the car to follow Nico.

Nico had just made it in the door when he heard gravel crunching behind him and footsteps on the marble floor in front of him. Then came the characteristic snap of a holster opening and the brush of metal against leather. Kriven grabbed his gun and made a quick half turn. He and Nico were now standing back to back.

"There are two of them between us and the car, Chief."

Nico kept his eyes on the person three feet in front of him who was pointing a Unique DES 69 at his chest. He recognized him immediately from the composite picture of the man who had threatened Bruno Guedj at the pharmacy.

"Chief of Police Nico Sirsky, with the Criminal Investigation Division," Nico said, raising his arms above his head. "This is Commander Kriven. We don't want any trouble. We're here to see Mr. Quere."

The man didn't say anything but tightened his grip on the gun. His forehead was sweaty.

Nico's body tensed. He calmed his breathing as his training kicked in. He needed some information. "Kriven, I believe our welcoming committee would like you to put your weapon down. Can you do that?"

"Sure, boss. The two kind men outside are just standing there, arms crossed."

Good, Nico thought. They're not armed.

The man cleared his throat. "Have him do it now," he said.

"Kriven, I suggest you do as he says. Put it on the floor, and kick it over to your left."

"Are you sure, boss? Right now?"

Kriven was buying his chief some time. Nico stabilized his center of gravity, bent his knees slightly, getting ready to shift to the right. His arms were still up above his head. He spread his hands out and waved them as if he were nervous. He was creating a distraction in his attacker's peripheral vision.

"The man has a gun pointed at me, Kriven, so yes, *now.*"

Nico heard the standard issue SP 2022 slide across the marble as Kriven veered out of the way. The man's eyes shifted, following the weapon. Nico had a split second to react. He swung his left arm down and grabbed the man's right hand, then twisted his wrist until the weapon was pointing at his assailant's throat. At the same time, he used his right arm to immobilize his attacker's other elbow with a lock. He applied pressure to the wrist until the man's grip loosened. Nico slid his hand up to grab the weapon.

Two clicks. Guns cocking. Gravel crunching. Nico turned his head and saw the two other heavies, weapons trained—one on Kriven, one on him. Straightening up to his full six-foot-two height, he kept the elbow lock, until the man howled. Nico hung on and swung the man around, shielding himself from the others.

"Now," Nico said, pushing the barrel under the man's chin, "call off the goon squad and take me to see Mr. Quere."

They entered the living room. Edward Quere was there. His back was turned to them, and he was staring out the window. Nico wondered for a moment if Quere had lost himself in the scenery, just as he had recently lost himself in the wintry window of the department store. A woman standing in front of a bookshelf filled with leather-bound classics watched them come in. His wife, Nico presumed.

Quere spun around. And Nico knew he would never forget what he saw. This wasn't the face of a man beguiled by the winter landscape outside. It was that of a man who was wasting away from the inside. His cheeks were hollow and his features emaciated. His eyes were two dark dry wells. His face mirrored the calamity in his life. In that second, Nico understood that Edward Quere, the respected boss and businessman, the power broker who often dined with the president, would not survive his daughter. He had opened Pandora's box. And Bruno Guedj had been a victim of his folly.

"What can I do for you?" Quere said with authority, his words echoing in the stillness of the room.

What arrogance, Nico thought. He had played in outside the boundaries. He had crossed the line. He had given orders to kill those who compromised his plans. Dr. Parize might have made the decision to flee his life and his responsibilities and reject the ethical rules of his profession, but Bruno Guedj had been nothing more than an innocent victim.

"For a start, you can tell us where you daughter is," Nico said calmly.

29

Nico heard sirens outside and movement behind him. He glanced around and saw the men in black regrouping as Kriven tensed to have his back.

"Stop," Edward Quere shouted to his bodyguards. "Idiots. It's over."

Quere's dogs had jumped to defend their master and had frozen at the sound of his voice. One did not resist Edward Quere. One obeyed.

"Edward," his wife pleaded.

He raised a hand to quiet her. Then she shot Nico a look that he found strange. It held more than despair. There was bitterness in her face with a hint of hatred.

"Where is Clarisse?" Nico asked.

"In the basement," Quere answered.

They crossed the sumptuously decorated ground floor. The walls were covered with paintings, some of which were worth a fortune. What use was such luxury, Nico thought, when one's child was desperately ill?

They opened a steel door and rushed down a flight of narrow, poorly lit stairs. At the bottom, a bright white light diffused a strange halo. Kriven hesitated, his hand on his gun. Nico knew the hospital stink had to be affecting him. The rest of his team was just behind them.

"No weapons," he ordered.

They were about to enter a ghostly world inhabited by a dying girl and a few apprentice sorcerers. That world had a name—the shadows—and a master—the devil. Nico refrained from telling Kriven that his gun would be superfluous.

They reached a vast tiled room with bright fluorescent lighting. A hospital bed drew their attention. Clarisse Quere lay there, emaciated. Nico could hardly bear to look at her. The nurse at the girl's bedside jumped at the sight of the men.

"These people are from the police," Edward Quere said. There was no emotion in his voice.

"Danièle Lemaire?" he asked.

She nodded, looking scared but remaining at the side of the only patient she had tended for many months.

"What's over there?" Nico asked, pointing to three doors in the room.

Kriven hurried in toward them, ready to find out.

"A private apartment, a bathroom adapted for my daughter, and a laboratory."

"Our daughter!" Helen Quere cried out, coming up from behind.

Nico saw Quere's posture droop. He walked over to the bed and touched Clarisse's forehead. She let out a nearly inaudible moan, her eyes closed for good.

"Go on," Nico ordered.

"You don't know what you're doing," Helen Quere hissed. A vein pulsed in her temple. "We're so close."

A man in a white coat appeared, hands cuffed behind his back. Captain Franck Plassard nudged him from behind.

"Professor Claude Janin," Plassard said. "He's got quite a lab here."

Nico sized up the scientist. "What have you done?"

"I perfected specific antibodies to fight T-cell lympho-blastic lymphoma!" Janin snapped. "The results are so promising, even the Nobel Prize wouldn't be enough recognition."

"We named it Clarimab," Helen Quere said. "'Clari' was for Clarisse, and 'mab' was for monoclonal antibody."

"Did it work?"

"There was a generalized viral infection after the treatment," Edward Quere said. "It's the end."

"For her!" Janin said.

"Claude!" Quere shouted. "That is my daughter. She's going to die, and I don't give a damn what becomes of your research. Do you understand?"

"But because of Claude, there's hope for many others," Danièle Lemaire said.

"Bullshit!" Helen Quere yelled, losing control. "Without our daughter, that means nothing to us."

The room fell silent. Nico took out his phone and made the call. "Dispatch? Get me an ambulance, please."

"You don't have the right to do that," Helen Quere screamed.

Nico ignored her. The paramedics would arrive any time now. He turned to Clarisse's mother and spoke to her with his characteristic calm. "Your husband arranged everything, of course. He had the means and the power, right? He had sacrificed so much to build his empire, stolen so much time from his family. He owed it to you. It never was his idea, was it?"

"He wouldn't have done anything," she spit out. "He would have just watched her die!"

"You threatened him."

"I was ready to leave with my daughter. Without any hesitation, and he wouldn't have seen us again. But believe me, it didn't take much to get him to come around. I was the one who took her to her ballet lessons and hired her tutors all those years when she was little, and he was busy building his empire. He always had plans for her, though. She was supposed to carry on after him. He was invested in her and cared about her every bit as much as I did. And in the end, he wasn't going to let her go. He was willing to do whatever it took to keep her alive."

"Take them away," Nico said.

His team escorted the Queres, Janin, and Lemaire to police headquarters, where they were taken into custody. It was the first step in a process that would inevitably lead to prison. The resolution of the molar mystery would be in the headlines first thing in the morning, and even bigger headlines would follow. The arrest of Edward Quere would rumble like thunder around the country. And everyone would know the details. Obsessed by his daughter's illness and willing to do everything in his power to save her, the businessman had stopped at nothing, not even murder. The man found in Dr. Parize's burned car had been a snare. But Quere couldn't control Parize, and then Bruno Guedj had threatened the entire operation. The CEO, backed against the wall, had gotten rid of them.

The forces of order prevailed. Strangely, Nico did not feel at ease. He had a bitter taste in his mouth.

The cancer had triggered all of this havoc. But the Queres and their willing—even eager—recruits had to take responsibility. Helen and Edward Quere had lost their moral compass, and the doctors had violated their ethics. Nico wondered what DrNo, Lol, and the others would have thought of that.

30

Nazebroc: How are things with you, Clarisse?

Stella1: I'm new to this blog, but I read your
story and wanted to wish you the very best.

Lol: Hey, girl, not sharing any news these days?

Pilou56: Hey, you. Where'd you go? You've gone
black. I hope you're taking care of yourself.

Océan2000: Hi, Stella1. Don't wear yourself
out. Clarisse hasn't shared a thing in weeks.

Lol: I'm starting to worry. Please,
give us some news.

DrNo: ALL is a bitch. Dammit! I told you so.

Lol: Bird of ill omen, don't you
have anything positive to say?

Bella: I know you're sad, Lol. Me too.

DrNo: Sissies. Go to hell.

Lol: Clarisse!! Come back.

Helios: DrNo was right. ALL got her.

Lol: It's been months since we've heard from her.

DrNo: Let it go, Grandma.

Bella: Bird of ill omen! Lol is the
best. And Clarisse is alive.

DrNo: You know what this bird has to say? That
he's got a cancer that's been eating away at him
for two years, and he knows it's the end. The END.
Even you sissies could lift me with one finger. I'm
a walking corpse—not even walking anymore.
I can't get out of bed, and I've got tubes going
everywhere. I'm screwed. I'm going to die. What
do you have to say about that? Nothing. Too bad I
won't be able to give you news of Clarisse from up
there, because that's where I'm headed, friends. So
Lol? You're not laughing anymore, huh. I'm crying.
Like Clarisse. In heaven, I'd like to kiss her on the
mouth. Make love to her. Think that's possible?

31

It was Wednesday, December 23. An impulse. Nico knocked on the door one more time. One last time.

"Hey, buddy."

It was Marcel, with his laughing eyes.

"Congratulations. Hats off to you. You're gettin' so much praise from all around, you must be looking for somewhere to hide. You found the right place. Your boss lady must be happy. What's her name again? Nicole Monthet, Montle?"

"Monthalet."

"That's it. Quite a woman. She owes you a big one. That's what she said in the papers."

Nico smiled.

"Glad you stopped by. The last time, I was sorry I didn't take you to the museum. You were in a hurry, though."

"To the museum?"

"That's right. It's something to see. And these days, most folks don't have the chance to visit, because it's closed. Follow me."

They climbed the huge staircase to the eighth floor, which was much quieter than the floors below. They walked past a gigantic painting of a young man who was slashed and bloody and tied to a rack. It was a grisly sight.

"That's Poirier dissecting. The Poirier Lab is named after him."

They walked into a room without knocking.

"John?" he called out.

"Yep, I'm here."

"I'm bringing you a living hero. Chief Sirsky."

A man who looked to be in his sixties, like Marcel, walked over to them. He had a willowy build and a gentle face. The window in his office offered an unobstructed view of the Eiffel Tower.

"John is a volunteer curator at the Delmas–Orfila–Rouviere Museum. Without him… Well, I have to show you."

Nico couldn't take his eyes off the glass case that held a lifelike *Sleeping Venus.* She was breathing.

"It's a unique masterpiece," John said. "It belongs to a rare collection of anatomical wax sculptures. She is so beautiful. You see how she breathes? Its creator, Dr. Spitzner, got a medal at the Vienna World's Fair in 1873 for the ingenious mechanism in the lady's chest that gives the impression that she is alive. It was really innovative in the nineteenth century."

"Show my friend around," Marcel said.

"This way."

In the hallway, Nico explored the strange exhibits: mummies of a father, mother, and their child found in the Paris Metro in 1900, a head dating from 1696 and presented to Louis XIV, the oldest known anatomical wax sculpture in France, molded skeletons, legs, arms, animals, and more.

"The Delmas–Orfila–Rouviere Museum comprises collections and specimens of both people and animals," John said. "The museum itself dates from the eighteenth century, but much of it was lost in subsequent centuries. Then, in the nineteen forties, Professor André Delmas was instrumental in bringing the museum back to life, so to speak. Today, it has nearly 6,000 items."

They walked through the dusty rooms, which were filled with cartons. Showcases displayed skeletons, from fetal to adult, various organs, and the skulls of torture victims.

"That skull belongs to Giuseppe Marco Fieschi, who conspired to kill King Louis-Philippe in 1835. In the nineteenth century, forensic scientists focused a lot on the behavior of murderers."

Nico stopped in front of the preserved skin of a thirty-five-year-old man and then in front of a wax representation of a woman undergoing a Caesarean section. Her hands and feet were bound, and the child was being extracted with hooks.

"There wasn't any anesthesia in the nineteenth century. Doctors used opium. Two-thirds of the women who underwent Caesarean sections died in childbirth. Did you notice that none of the wax figures show any pain? Here's an anatomical Venus, which can be taken apart in forty-four pieces. It comes from the Spitzner collection. It was an attraction at fairs for a long time."

"It all looks abandoned."

"The museum has been closed to the public for some time now. Every year, the school takes away a little more of our space, which explains the boxes. I only see students doing research these days."

"But why?"

"There's no money for upkeep. Priorities are elsewhere. We're looking for a buyer, but so far, one hasn't shown up."

Nico sighed. "So meticulously collected and cared for, and still, there's just so much you can control. The people who hold the purse strings don't have the same vision for this place that you have. It's like so much else in our lives. Elements beyond our control often get the better of our hopes and ambitions."

"It'd be nice, wouldn't it, if you could get someone in accounting to cook the books a little and filter some of that cash to this museum," Marcel said. "But that wouldn't be right, would it?"

"Sometimes you have to accept what you can't change. As wonderful as this museum is, it will probably remain closed."

"Aha. We've saved the best for last," Marcel said.

The showcase displayed castings of two human brains.

"The statesman Léon Gambetta."

"Nine hundred cubic centimeters. That's the equivalent of a five-year-old child's brain," John said.

Marcel laughed. "Conclusion: just because you've got a big head, that doesn't mean you're smart."

"And there you have Vacher's brain," John said.

"Joseph Vacher, the serial killer?" Nico asked.

"Exactly."

The two hemispheres were enormous.

"Now, he did have a huge brain, but that didn't prove he was smart, either," John said. "We'd call it a pathological brain."

The tour ended, and Marcel accompanied Nico back down the stairs.

"Isn't that museum a gas?"

"I agree."

"I spend more time talking to dead folks than living ones. It's the job. But I have the feeling that you've got something on your mind."

Nico stopped at the bottom of the staircase. Just a few students were coming and going. It was Christmas vacation.

"Clarisse Quere died this morning," he said.

32

Caroline had slipped on her lace panties and was hooking her bra. Nico never tired of watching her do these simple things. She had so much grace and sensuality, it took all his discipline to keep from grabbing her, kissing the back of her neck, and telling her how beautiful she was.

Caroline gave him a mischievous smile. She made her way over to him like a cat. She buttoned his light-blue shirt and tied his tie, while rubbing against him and pretending to be sweet and innocent. And there he was—six-foot-two and all muscle—feeling like a wobbly teenager. He stopped moving, his heart beating hard in his chest. He felt hot. Caroline slipped her fingers through his blond hair and slowly pressed her lips against his. They kissed for a long time. He could think of only one thing: making love.

She pulled away. "Darling, we're going to be late," she murmured.

The angel had slipped from his grasp. She put on a magnificent black silk dress and asked him to clasp her pearl necklace. He had to put out the fire that was still smoldering. Suddenly, she turned to him and gave him an intense, troubled look. A shiver ran up Nico's spine. What was happening?

"I have something for you."

She dug around in her bag and handed him a small box wrapped in Santa paper. He undid the ribbon and clumsily ripped at the paper. The Santas seemed to be mocking him. He opened the box, and his eyes widened. Was he understanding this correctly?

"If you still want to," she said, shyly.

The box held a magnificent key ring with a multicolored heart.

"Don't move," he said. He rushed out of the bedroom and returned with the key. "This is for you."

He slipped the key onto the key ring and gave it to her. It was official. This home was their home. He took Caroline in his arms and held her tight. "I love you so much," he whispered in her ear.

"And I love you."

"Dad! Caroline! Are you ready?"

Dimitri was eager to leave. "Where are the gifts, Dad?"

"In Santa's bag, of course!"

"Aha. You put them in the trunk of the car, right?"

"No, my son. You must believe in the magic of Christmas," Nico said in Russian.

In truth, he had dropped them off at his sister's house the day before.

"But I do believe."

"Can we go, boys?" Caroline said, smiling.

"Madame," Nico replied, presenting his arm.

She took his arm and nodded. Dimitri laughed and closed the door behind them.

Paris, dressed in its Christmas finery, was ready for the festivities. A thousand lights twinkled in the city. Covered with a blanket of snow, the Luxembourg Gardens gleamed in the moonlight.

Anya opened the door of the apartment on the Rue Soufflot. It didn't take Dimitri more than a second to run off and join the gang of kids in one of the bedrooms.

A voice came from behind them. "Merry Christmas!"

Alexis was returning from the wine cellar, his arms full of bottles. Nico's physician brother-in-law was a passionate seaman, having sailed both the Atlantic and the Pacific, and a connoisseur of wines.

"A Château-Chalon!" Nico said, full of enthusiasm.

Alexis had introduced him to this white wine from the Jura a few years earlier. The elixir had an aroma of walnuts and dried fruit, and Nico imagined that it would have been relished at the table of Tsar Nicolas II.

Caroline disappeared into the kitchen to set down the traditional *bûche de Noël* and hide the candy. Otherwise the younger crowd would devour it before the meal.

The doorbell resonated throughout the apartment. There was activity in the vestibule. Nico recognized the voice of his friend Alexandre Becker. They greeted each other with a friendly embrace. The magistrate's two children ran off to find Dimitri and his cousins. His wife was already in the kitchen, praising Tanya's dishes. While Alexis put the finishing touches on the appetizers, Becker and Nico retreated to the Christmas tree.

"Are you happy?" Becker asked, smiling.

"You could say that," Nico responded, thinking about Caroline's key ring.

"An investigation well done," the magistrate said.

He was referring to the molar mystery, which was now the Edward Quere case. "Everyone involved is locked up, but people are still talking about it. It's affected the whole world of medical research."

"There are good people fighting heart and soul to defeat cancer. A few black sheep can't detract from their heroic work."

"In any case, your intuition never ceases to amaze me. It's a real gift you have there."

"Ho, ho, ho. Boys, it's Christmas," Alexis said. "Forget about work. I'm opening the Champagne."

Tanya called them to the table. Anya asked for silence. Tasting caviar required contemplation. Russians claimed the protein-rich food was an aphrodisiac, that it improved eyesight and slowed the effects of alcohol. Not that any caviar aficionados wanted to do that, considering all the vodka they enjoyed consuming with it. Tanya served the blinis, and Alexis brought out the ice-cold vodka. Anya started humming "Kalinka," a traditional—and naughty—Russian song.

Raising his glass, Alexis responded with a traditional Breton song. He wouldn't be outdone. "Or these Russians are going to eat us alive. Sooner or later, they'll be trying to put a tsar on the French throne."

"Nico I," Dimitri cried out.

"You see, all fanatics!" Alexis shouted.

They all laughed. Nico was rubbing Caroline's thigh under the table. He was also thinking about Jacqueline and André, his former in-laws, and about Sylvie. The next day, on Christmas, he had planned to drive his son to Saujon so Dimitri could celebrate Christmas with his mother, but Dimitri had refused. "Dad, this is between me and Mom. Let it go," he had said.

Alexis turned to Dimitri. "So, you're a few months away from high school. Do you have an idea what you want to do later?"

"Of course."

"And that is?" Becker asked.

Dimitri blushed. "The National Police Academy."

Nico's jaw dropped open. "But the job is…"

His mother interrupted. "What? Dangerous? Dimitri's not ten anymore. If he wants to play gendarmes and robbers, that's his choice. Now tell him what's in your heart, which is the only thing worth saying."

Nico found himself catapulted into the past, his mind swirling. He cleared his throat and hesitated. And then he did exactly what his father had done.

"I love you, son."

"Case closed," Anya proclaimed.

Gifts were piled under the tree, waiting for their recipients. Anya picked up the first present.

"A book."

"Why, it's a guidebook to Ukraine," Tanya said, holding up the present that she had just opened. "What—"

"Plane tickets," her mother cried out. "For Kiev! In February."

"We're going as a family," Nico said. "Ten days. Kiev, Odessa, the Black Sea."

"Oh, Nico, I didn't think I'd see it before I died."

"Who said anything about dying? Besides, we'll have a doctor on board."

"*Schastlivogo Rozhdestva*!" Dimitri said.

"Oh yes!" his grandmother said, thrilled to hear her grandson wishing her a Merry Christmas in her native tongue.

Nico suddenly had a memory of his son on his tricycle. The boy was hardly more than a toddler. Nico was running after Dimitri's colored balloons as they took off toward the sky, and his son was squealing with delight. Life passed so quickly. Too quickly.

EPILOGUE

Agence France Press Dispatch – January 25 12:33
Reference: DAT0508 3 Y F 0150 FRA/AFP-AG16

Paris, January 25 (AFP)
Edward Quere Attempts Suicide

Held in solitary confinement at the Santé Prison
in Paris, well-known businessman Edward
Quere attempted suicide this morning. He had
taken an unknown quantity of opioid painkillers. The guards were quick to respond, and a
medical team intervened immediately, saving
his life. He will remain under medical watch
for forty-eight hours. Prison officials said that
Quere told them he would try again. He said that
he wanted to join his daughter, Clarisse, who
died last month. An investigation is under way
to determine how Quere obtained the pills.

Thank you for reading Crossing the Line.

We invite you to share your thoughts and reactions on Goodreads and your favorite social media and retail platforms.

We appreciate your support.

Acknowledgments

The mystery is solved, and the book closes. Now comes the time to express my gratitude and my friendship to all those who accompanied me on this adventure:

Édith Bordereaux, administrative manager of the Paris Descartes University Body Donation Center.

Dr. David Corège, chief rescue-squad medical officer in the Saône-et-Loire, and forensics expert with the court of Dijon.

Christian Flaesch, police commissioner and former section chief of the Paris Criminal Investigation Division.

Maurice Harasse, anatomy lab technician at the Paris Descartes University.

Frédéric Péchenard, national police prefect and former chief of the Paris Criminal Investigation Division.

Patrick Prieux, dental surgeon with a passion for anatomy.

Christine Sagnal, with the National Police Forensics Institute, responsible for communications and training at the Lyons forensics laboratory.

Dr. Bruno Salles, hemato-oncologist at the Chalon-sur-Saône Hospital.

Hubert Weigel, director of the Compagnies Républicaines de Sécurité for the director of the National Police Forensics Institute and all its services.

A special mention goes to Dr. Lionel Yon, an orthopedic surgeon, and to Lilas Seewald, my editor at Fayard Noir.

ABOUT THE AUTHOR

Writing has always been a passion for Frédérique Molay. She graduated from France's prestigious Science Po and began her career in politics and the French administration. She worked as chief of staff for the deputy mayor of Saint-Germain-en-Laye and then was elected to the local government in Saône-et-Loire. Meanwhile, she spent her nights pursuing the passion she had nourished since penning her first novel at the age of eleven. After *The 7ʰ Woman* took France by storm, Frédérique Molay dedicated her life to writing and raising her three children. She has five books to her name, with three in the Paris Homicide series.

ABOUT THE TRANSLATOR

Anne Trager has lived in France for more than twenty-six years, working in translation, publishing, and communications. In 2011, she woke up one morning and said, "I just can't stand it anymore. There are way too many good books being written in France not reaching a broader audience." That's when she founded Le French Book to translate some of those books into English. The company's motto is, "If we love it, we translate it," and Anne loves a good police procedural.

ABOUT LE FRENCH BOOK

Le French Book is a New York–based publisher specializing in great reads from France. As founder Anne Trager says, "There is a very vibrant, creative culture in France. Our vocation is to bring France's best mysteries, thrillers, novels, and short stories to new readers across the English-speaking world."

www.lefrenchbook.com

Discover more books from

Le French Book

The Paris Lawyer by **Sylvie Granotier**
A psychological thriller set between the sophisticated corridors of the Paris courts and a small backwater in central France, where rolling hills and quiet country life hide dark secrets.
www.theparislawyer.com

The Winemaker Detective Series
by Jean-Pierre Alaux and Noël Balen
A total Epicurean immersion in French countryside and gourmet attitude with two expert winemakers turned amateur sleuths gumshoeing around wine country. Already translated: *Treachery in Bordeaux, Grand Cru Heist* and *Nightmare in Burgundy.*
www.thewinemakerdetective.com

The Greenland Breach by **Bernard Besson**
The Arctic ice caps are breaking up. Europe and the East Coast of the United States brace for a tidal wave. A team of freelance spies face a merciless war for control of discoveries that will change the future of humanity.
www.thegreenlandbreach.com

The Bleiberg Project by **David Khara**
Are Hitler's atrocities really over? Find out in this adrenaline-pumping ride to save the world from a conspiracy straight out of the darkest hours of history.
www.thebleibergproject.com

CPSIA information can be obtained at www.ICGtesting.com
Printed in the USA
BVOW04*1027030914

364228BV00001B/1/P

9 781939 474162